MOTHMAN'S CURSE

CHRISTINE HAYES

MOTHMAN'S CURSE

Pictures by
JAMES K. HINDLE

SQUARE
FISH

Roaring Brook Press • New York

SQUARE FISH

An Imprint of Macmillan
175 Fifth Avenue
New York, NY 10010
mackids.com

Our books may be purchased in bulk for promotional, educational, or business
use. Please contact your local bookseller or the Macmillan Corporate
and Premium Sales Department at (800) 221-7945 ext. 5442 or by
e-mail at MacmillanSpecialMarkets@macmillan.com.

Library of Congress Cataloging-in-Publication Data

Hayes, Christine, 1972–
  Mothman's curse / Christine Hayes ; illustrated by James Hindle.
    pages cm
  Summary: "When Josie and her brother Fox discover the truth behind
the legend of the Mothman, they must stop a disaster in order to break
the curse that has been afflicting their town"—Provided by publisher.
  ISBN 978-1-250-07989-3 (paperback)   ISBN 978-1-62672-028-2 (ebook)
  [1. Mothman—Fiction.   2. Blessing and cursing—Fiction.
3. Supernatural—Fiction.   4. Brothers and sisters—Fiction.   5. Single-
parent families—Fiction.   6. Family life—Ohio—Fiction.   7. Ohio—
Fiction.   8. Horror stories.]   I. Hindle, James K., illustrator.   II. Title.
  PZ7.1.H394Mot 2015
  [Fic]—dc23

2014047412

Originally published in the United States by Roaring Brook Press
First Square Fish Edition: 2016
Book designed by Andrew Arnold
Square Fish logo designed by Filomena Tuosto

1 3 5 7 9 10 8 6 4 2

AR: 4.6 / LEXILE: 690L

For Bryce

WHEN YOU LIVE IN THE MOST HAUNTED town in America, you've heard most every ghost story that's ever been spun about your corner of the world: the tumbledown houses, the shadowed cemeteries and wandering souls. Whether you believe the stories or not, you respect them—just in case.

Plenty of places *claim* to be the most haunted. But Athens, Ohio, has something those other places don't.

Mothman.

He's every bit as repulsive as he sounds: a dark, hulking figure, seven feet tall, with ragged, brittle wings and burning red eyes.

Technically he belongs to Point Pleasant, West Virginia, where dozens died when the Silver Bridge collapsed in '67. Scores of people spotted Mothman in the year before the disaster. No one knew if he was there to help or harm. He's been called a ghost, an alien, and a monster. I've always thought *death omen* described him best.

Point Pleasant is forty miles from Athens. Mothman was never ours to claim, and I was glad.

Until this spring, when Mothman claimed Athens instead.

* * *

Dad's voice rose and fell, hummingbird quick, his mustached mouth crowding the microphone. "Up next we have a food processor, that's a Sunrise food processor, make you some nice coleslaw right there. Do I hear a dollar bill, dollar bill? Now two, two, two dollar, two dollar, and who'll give me three?"

I stood in the back corner, sizing up the shoppers. Sharp-eyed regulars hovered around the tables of merchandise in their T-shirts and trucker hats, sussing out valuable pieces. Clusters of stooped men in overalls debated the odds of another wet spring, their work boots squeaking on the auction floor. Several dozen customers perched in plastic chairs. They hugged cardboard boxes close to their bodies with hands that were callused and winter-pale, itching to fill them with what my younger brother Fox likes to call secondhand swag.

The great Fox Fletcher himself prowled the room. I spotted an easy mark at Table 3: a round, middle-aged woman in pink capris and a tennis visor. She was admiring a figurine trimmed in fake gold—a terrier with a huge bow on its head.

I caught my brother's eye, tipping my chin toward the lady in pink. Fox nodded; he'd spotted her, too.

Time to go to work.

He sidled up beside her, batting guileless green eyes. I slipped closer to listen in.

"You must be new in town," Fox was saying. "We know most of the regulars." He nodded at the milling shoppers. "You're a lot younger and . . . truthfully, a much better dresser than our usual crowd."

"Well, aren't you a smooth talker?" She propped a hand on her hip, pressed the other hand to her blushing face. "I happen to be visiting my cousin and her family, the Lesters."

"Oh, sure. Mr. Lester teaches at the middle school, right? I'll be starting there next fall."

"That's right."

"So are you here for the ghosts, then?"

"Ghosts?"

"That's why most people come to Athens." He pulled a stack of leaflets from his pocket and handed her a brochure titled "Haunted Tours of Athens County" from the top of the pile. "Some people say the town sits right on top of a spectral vortex. A doorway for the weird."

"Oh, I don't really believe in ghosts."

"A skeptic, huh? That's okay. Most people are." He held up the next brochure in the pile. "That's because they only visit the touristy sites: the mental asylum, Wilson Hall, the Weeping Angel. But if you want the real story, this map has sites only the locals know about. Ghost stories that go back generations, with real eye-witness sightings. The best of the best."

She took the flyer and unfolded it to reveal a hand-drawn map with blocks of careful printing in a child's hand. "Did you do this? What a lot of time it must have taken."

I crossed my fingers and toes, knowing Fox's next lines would be a tough sell.

Fox shrugged and kept his gaze on the ground. "My sister and I did them together to earn a few extra dollars. Our dad runs this place. He says we're too young to be of much use, but money's been real tight." He shuffled his foot, drawing attention to the ragged hole in the toe of his sneakers—the hole I'd watched him put there with a pair of scissors. Fox chewed his lip a little. Hung his head. Let his shoulders slump just so . . .

"I'd love to buy one! What do you charge?"

"Just one dollar, ma'am."

"Oh, pish. Look at all this work you went to. So creative!" She pulled a ten-dollar bill from her fanny pack. "Here, now. You take this and share it with your sister, all right? The world needs more young people like you."

I rolled my eyes, feeling a familiar twinge of envy and awe. Still, ten bucks was a good start for the day. I didn't always agree with Fox's methods, but it was hard to argue with his results.

"That's very generous, ma'am. Thank you," Fox said. "By the way, that's a good piece you're looking at. Would fetch a nice resale price."

"You think so?"

"You hang around here long enough, you get an eye for things."

"That's real sweet of you. Thanks for the tip, young man. And the map."

He flashed a smile, a deadly one-two punch of twin dimples and perfect teeth. "It's Fox. Fox Fletcher. Happy to help, ma'am. I also happen to specialize in haunted objects, if you know anyone who's in the market." He strolled his way toward the exit, slowing down when something on Table 6 caught his eye. In one quick motion, he tucked the item under his T-shirt. Then, whistling, he breezed on out into the chilly March morning.

"Fox," I murmured, the word sounding like a sigh. "What are you up to now?" I ducked out, too, determined not to let him stray from The Plan.

I fell into step beside him. "What did you take in there? You know it has to go back."

"I'll take it back. Relax, would you? How about a thank-you for my flawless performance?"

"Speaking of which, can we *please* redo those maps on the computer? They look like a four-year-old drew them. It's embarrassing."

"That's the whole point, Josie. They generate sympathy. Sympathy earns us more money."

I flipped open my notebook and slid a pencil from behind my ear. "So what's our total so far? Was that a ten she gave you?"

"Nope. Just a five."

"Uh-huh. How about the truth this time?"

He breathed a long-suffering sigh. "I'm tired of pooling every penny we make. Just once I'd like a Snickers bar and a Saturday morning without you and your notebook."

"We all agreed on this. I have it in writing. Permanent marker, Fox."

"I don't see you in there earning anything."

"Not my fault you're the best liar in the family."

"Fox! Josie!"

Our little brother Mason, a seven-year-old human wrecking ball, trotted over. He danced at Fox's other side, kicking up mud, his feet in constant motion. "What's under your shirt? Did you find something good? Let's see. I wanna see."

"What makes you think I found anything?"

"Foooooooox! What'd you find?"

"You mean this?" He unveiled his prize with an extra flourish. It was a Polaroid camera—decades old, dusty, and dented, nestled inside a worn leather case. The camera was a boxy, clunky thing, but it had a certain charm, a kind of techno-geek chic. And in Fox's hands, any old piece of junk suddenly seemed worthy of attention.

"Wow!" Mason tried to grab it away. "Can I take it apart?"

Fox settled the leather strap across his chest. "Nope."

I wrinkled my nose, pretending not to be interested. "What do you want that old thing for?"

"I like it. Besides, they won't miss it. It'll be hours before Dad gets around to Table Six. By then I'll have it back, safe and sound. Say cheese, Josie."

"There's not even any film in—"

With a click and a whir, the camera spit out a white square of photo paper.

"The film's so old it won't even—"

The square resolved into a picture of my horribly freckled face.

I grabbed it and stuffed it in my back pocket, ignoring Fox's grin.

"Can I try, Fox?" Mason said. "How does it work?"

"It's an instant camera, short stuff. The picture pops out as soon as you press the button." Fox handed the camera over for Mason to inspect. "Careful now."

Mason examined every inch of it. "Where's the view screen? Is there a memory card?"

Fox took the camera back. "It's older than that. Cameras didn't have those things years ago."

Mason's stomach rumbled loud and long, sounding like a question at the end. "I'm hungry. Can't we cancel The Plan, just for today? We haven't been to the corner store in weeks. Pleeeeaaase, Josie?"

Fox started in, too. "Pleeeeaaase?"

Being in charge wasn't as peachy as it sounded—not with two kid brothers who constantly ganged up on me. I sighed. "Go on, then!"

Mason tugged on my hand. "Aren't you coming, Josie?"

"Nah," Fox said. "She's afraid of Old Man Hicks."

"I am not," I lied. The crusty old man who ran the corner store hated everyone and everything. I wasn't much in the mood to get yelled at for the sake of a measly candy bar.

"Hold my camera?" Fox thrust the case into my hands. Then he and Mason took off running before I could protest.

"Get me a Hershey bar, without nuts!" I shouted after them. "And it's not your camera!"

I kicked a stone and watched it skip along the gravel driveway, feeling guilty about choosing candy over my duty as Plan Enforcer.

To put it simply, The Plan involved saving up enough money to get us to the state fair in Columbus—home of the junior auctioneer's bid call competition.

Our great-grandpa Henry started Fletcher Auctions. The same house, same junk, same life got passed down from one generation of Fletchers to the next. Dad handled estates all over Athens County, selling the stuff people left behind when they passed away.

On Saturdays, it seemed as if half the town hung around our place instead of their own perfectly good houses. Between the rubberneckers and the bargain hunters, it was hard to get a moment's peace.

Enter The Plan. When Momma was alive, our family would load up the car and head to the state fair every summer. Momma's apricot jam always won the first-place ribbon. Dad's skill with a rifle won us armfuls of stuffed toys on the midway. My brothers and I binged on funnel cakes and cotton candy. And Momma always said that when Fox was old enough, we'd sign him up for the junior bid call competition.

But then she got sick. Aunt Barb and Uncle Bill moved

into the apartment above the garage to help out, and everything changed.

We hadn't been to the fair since Momma died three years ago. Dad said it didn't feel right going without her. All he ever wanted to do was work.

I missed Momma's too-loud laugh, and her smothering hugs, and the way she'd tuck my hair behind my ear and tell me my freckles were as beautiful as the stars in the sky. She was fearless and fun, the roller coaster to Dad's sure, steady Ferris wheel. I knew it would make her sad that we'd stopped going to Columbus. Plus Fox was turning twelve in June—old enough to compete at the fair. Maybe somehow, if we made it to the competition, she'd look down from heaven and see that her family was doing okay.

I didn't have any special talents, not like Fox or Dad or Momma or even Mason, who could eat a dozen hot dogs in three minutes flat. I wouldn't be winning any ribbons at the fair. But I could at least try to get us there. If that meant making sure we pooled every penny for the trip, then that was what I'd do.

All because Fox—as you might expect—was born to be an auctioneer.

Fox could sell water to a drowning man, could turn trash into a treasure map. Aside from the money we made from clueless customers, we held kids-only auctions twice a month with items we'd scrounged and salvaged and even a few we'd rescued from the garbage heap. Every kid within five miles knew that a Fox Fletcher auction was not to be missed—especially since Fox claimed that half the items were haunted. He got to practice his calling skills and earn money for The Plan at the same time.

I saw my brothers disappear into the corner store a quarter mile down the road. I took the camera from its case and looked it over, tracing the lines and curves with one finger.

I glanced around to see if anyone was nearby, then lifted the viewer to my eye and pressed the button, snapping a picture of the muddy pasture.

As I waited for the image to sharpen, a dark, blurred shadow began to form in the center of the picture. I squinted and held the photo inches from my nose . . .

. . . And jumped when the shadow became a black-and-white image of a man staring grim-faced into the camera.

He wore thick, ugly glasses and a suit with a wide tie, like the kind in Grandpa's wedding photos. And he looked so sad I nearly burst into tears on the spot.

I stared. The field in the photograph looked normal, its colors unchanged. Only the man—the one who shouldn't be there—lacked any trace of color. My gaze traveled from the picture to the empty field in front of me, then back to the picture again. Fox had set this up somehow—I just knew it. I gave the camera a good shake, as if to dislodge whatever gadget he'd rigged to cause the unsettling image.

I saw the boys leave the store and head in my direction.

When Mason spotted me, he started to run. Fox chased him, the crisp air turning their cheeks rosy, their laughter floating ahead of them on the breeze.

"Are you taking pictures, Josie?" Mason mumble-shouted when he reached me, his mouth already stuffed with jawbreakers.

Fox pulled the photo from my hands. "Josie, who is this?"

"Like you don't know," I said. "Some joke, Fox. You shouldn't be messing with stuff that's already up for sale."

"What? I've never touched the camera before today." He took a closer look at the photo. "You're telling me you took a picture of the field and this is what came out?" Fox's usual cool exterior slipped a little. He licked his lips. Even knowing what a good actor he was, I found myself believing him. "Must be a trick camera," he said. "Or maybe an old image got transposed somehow. Josie, let me see that first photo I took of you."

I took it from my pocket and turned it over.

There I was in full-color, freckled glory, and there was the man—same stark expression, black and white from head to toe—standing right behind me.

I yelped and flung the picture away. My skin felt too tight, the air too thick.

"Who is he?" Mason wondered.

Fox bent to pick up the fallen photo. "It has to be some kind of trick."

"Now can I take it apart?" Mason said.

Fox and I answered together, "No!"

"Try another picture, Fox," I said, handing him the camera. Maybe my voice shook a little, and maybe Fox's hands did, too, but he covered it well, careful not to let Mason see.

He spun a slow circle and stopped, facing our property in the distance: our house; the barn; the long, low building that served as the auction floor; the few hundred cars and trucks belonging to customers, parked in uneven rows along the muddy lot.

And not a person in sight.

Fox raised the camera and pressed the button. A picture fell into his outstretched hand. I watched over his shoulder to see what would appear. Mason stood on his tiptoes. We held our breath.

The details sharpened into focus. It was our property, all right—with one key difference: the drab figure of our mystery man, close enough to count the smudges on his glasses.

I shivered.

Fox kept his cool, though only just. "Josie, how much money do we have saved?"

I checked my notebook. "Eighty-seven dollars and twenty-two cents—minus whatever you just spent on candy."

"We have to buy this camera."

I RAN TO THE HOUSE AND UP THE STAIRS TO MY room to grab the lockbox with our savings inside. I fished the key from the chain around my neck and dragged the box from the darkest corner of my closet. The Polaroids went into the box, facedown. The money went into my jeans pocket.

Kneeling there on the closet floor, I felt a draft creep in through the open door and curl around me like smoke. I looked down to see my hand halfway to the lockbox again, itching to turn over the photos for one more look. My fingers twitched as I fought the urge. Before I could stop myself, I reached in and flipped over the top photo.

Sadness filled me as I stared at the man, his edges slightly smudged as if drawn with charcoal. My throat tightened. I couldn't shake the feeling that he was looking back at me. The sadness sharpened into worry and fear. Who was he? What did he want?

I dropped the photo into the box, slammed the lid, and hurried back to the auction floor.

Things looked much the same as they had earlier, but Tables 1 through 4 were empty. Many of the customers' cardboard boxes were full.

Dad's voice raced along, hawking a woman's pillbox hat.

Fox had returned the camera to its proper spot on Table 6. He stood close by, not guarding it exactly, but sending frequent glances in its direction. His posture screamed *relaxed*, both elbows resting on the table behind him, head cocked as if watching the bidding unfold with wide-eyed attention, as if he hadn't seen the same thing every Saturday since birth.

He was, in fact, looking for someone to help us. Once items made it to the auction floor, we weren't supposed to touch them. Dad took the rules seriously and made sure we did the same. Fox never should have messed with the camera in the first place. Bidding was our best option now, but only grown-ups were allowed to bid. We could ask one of the regulars to bid for us—brothers Carl and Joe, or Mr. Leonard, who owned the drugstore downtown. But we didn't want any questions. And if one of the regulars bid on something,.you could bet the others would decide it was valuable and start a bidding war.

I watched Fox consider and reject a dozen people in the room before he noticed pink capris lady. She'd won her dog figurine—its head peeked out from the fanny pack around her middle.

Fox glanced at me; I nodded. We both approached her together, motioning her over for a hushed conversation at the back of the room.

"You got your dog," Fox said with an easy smile. "Good for you. Hope it didn't set you back too much."

She beamed. "Three dollars! Isn't he just the cutest? I can't believe there weren't more bidders!"

"This is my sister, Josie."

The woman took my hand, embracing it with both of her own. "Hey there, Josie. My name's Amelia. What a charming big brother you have!"

"I'm older," I blurted.

"Oh, I'm sorry, hon. Isn't this just the most fun ever? 'Course you two get to live it every week."

"Yes, ma'am." I didn't have the slightest idea how to ask this stranger for a favor.

Fox plunged right in. "Ms. Amelia, may we ask for your help?"

"Ask away."

"There's a camera we'd like to buy, over there, but we're not allowed to bid. We have money," he added quickly. "If you'd be willing . . ."

"Say no more. I'll be happy to bid for you. It's rather exciting, isn't it? I can't even understand what the auctioneer is saying."

"It may be another hour or two before they get to it. If there's somewhere else you need to be . . ."

"Nonsense. I haven't had this much fun in ages. You two sit tight and leave it to me."

Fox started fidgeting. His eyes shifted sideways and back, sideways and back.

His conscience was kicking in.

"The thing is, ma'am, I may not have been totally truthful before. About the dog being valuable."

She winked. "I know. Don't let the fanny pack fool you. This old broad's not as gullible as she looks." She patted the figurine. "I love it anyway. And I can appreciate two savvy kids looking to make a few bucks."

Fox grinned. I didn't. If I'd been the one who'd conned her, no doubt she'd have marched out the door in a huff.

We waited. Items were sold and collected one by one. I leaned against the wall, drumming my fingers in rhythm with Dad's voice.

Finally it was time.

"And here we have a leather and chrome Polaroid SX-Seventy Land Camera, a great piece right there, comes with its own carrying case. Bill, any film in that camera?"

Uncle Bill doubled as a sort of awkward spokesmodel for the auction items. Imagine Frankenstein with gray, wavy hat hair and a few too many apple fritters in his belly, and you get Uncle Bill. He stood in his plaid shirt and Wranglers, stooping to make himself smaller, holding up the camera for all to see. He paused to remove the bottom panel, peek inside, and shake his head. No film.

Fox and I exchanged startled glances. No *film*?

Dad started up his spiel again. "Okay, then, still a true piece of Americana right there. Let's hear ten, ten, ten dollar, ten dollar, ten, and thank you very much, sir, and fifteen, fifteen, fifteen, fifteen? And fifteen! Now twenty . . ."

Amelia raised her hand. She looked at us, eyebrows aloft. Fox nodded his approval. I chewed on my pencil. Maybe we used up all the film. Maybe it fell out. There had to be an explanation.

Fox gave the stink-eye to the man bidding against Amelia. What did the guy want with a useless old camera, anyway? Well, useless as far as he knew.

Another bidder joined in and the price jumped to thirty dollars. An empty pit churned where my stomach was supposed to be. I was glad I hadn't had time to eat my Hershey bar.

Amelia bid thirty-five dollars, then forty-five. Sixty dollars. I murdered that poor pencil, waiting and worrying, until the other bidders finally shook their heads and withdrew.

"That's sixty, sixty dollars, once, twice, and sold to the lady in pink."

Aunt Barb, seated next to Dad at the podium, recorded the transaction in the logbook. Amelia held up her bidder's card: number 98. Uncle Bill carried the camera over and placed it in her outstretched hands.

I slumped, overcome by a mix of relief and buyer's remorse. There went a good chunk of our hard-earned money—our trip money—and for what?

A broken-down clunker of a camera that took pictures without film. Creepy pictures of a creepy man that sent chills down my spine and right back up again.

I couldn't shake the sudden, sinking feeling that our sixty dollars had bought us a lot more trouble than we'd bargained for.

* * *

We took our new camera someplace where we could count on total privacy: an old wood shack we called the Cave. Hunched under a clump of trees behind our house, it made the perfect base of operations for Fox's auctions. We'd sent Mason there before the bidding to wait while we secured the camera. The kid had plenty of useful skills; he just had no poker face.

We found him playing with an old calculator, or what was left of it. Its pieces were strewn across the card table in the middle of the room. Candy wrappers littered the floor. When he saw us, he nearly fell out of his chair, demanding to know what he'd missed.

Fox chose a seat at the table. I took the time to check for cobwebs by flailing my arms in a few wild circles before sitting down beside Mason. We were locked in constant battle with the spiders for ownership of the Cave. I didn't want them getting any ideas about landing in my hair.

Fox set the camera on the table and we all stared at it awhile. Then Fox picked it up again and checked to confirm what Uncle Bill had already shown a roomful of customers: no film. "How is this thing taking pictures?" he muttered. He poked and prodded, but the camera seemed completely ordinary.

Mason crunched on a jawbreaker right in my ear. He flexed his fingers as if he wanted to snatch the camera out of Fox's hands.

I stared him down. "Don't you get any ideas. You're not taking it apart," I told him, just as Fox turned the camera on himself and snapped a close-up of his face.

"What are you doing?" I said.

"I dare the guy to show up in a picture of my nose. In fact . . . " He snapped a photo of the table, and another of the ceiling, and a few more random shots before I thought to jump up and grab the camera away. Leave it to Fox to get into a throwdown with a ghostly image.

"Fox, stop it!" Maybe it was just a trick camera, or

maybe it was something more, but taunting it didn't seem like the smartest way to find out.

Fox stood up, too. "What? It's not like there's any film."

"Well, you never know when it might stop working. We spent *sixty dollars* on that thing."

"Not much we can do about that now. Although . . . " His eyes got that greedy glaze. It didn't hurt that they were the exact color of a dollar bill. "We could probably get our money back and then some if *we* auctioned it. What kid wouldn't kill for a haunted camera?"

"Forget it. How can you even think about selling it?"

"Who says we have to sell *this* camera? I bet Dad has dozens of old cameras around the house. I dream up a few new ghost stories, doctor a couple of photographs . . . "

"Fox."

His voice got all hushed and breathy. "I can't believe I never thought of selling cameras before. They'd be the crown jewels of Fletcher's Haunted Artifacts."

"Fox!"

"Give me one auction and I could make it all back," he muttered. He gathered the pictures he'd snapped and fanned them out on the table. We leaned in close, but not too close, waiting for the images to take shape.

Mason slipped his hand into mine. "All right, Mr. Tall, Dark, and Scary," Fox whispered. "Show your face."

Another few seconds and we had our answer. In every photo: creepy man, creepy man, creepy man. Sometimes front and center, sometimes lurking in the background, but always there, always with the same expression. We had half a dozen pictures of the saddest person in the world.

Fox released a slow breath. He picked up a photo and squinted at it, his arm not quite steady. "That's it, then. It has to be a trick camera. He shows up every time, looks the same every time." He was about to toss the picture down when he stopped short, his fingers gripping the edge with crushing force, face stricken. "Did you see that?"

"See what?" I said.

"His lips moved."

Mason tightened his hold on my hand.

"They did not," I insisted. "Quit messing around."

Fox shoved the picture under my nose. Sure enough, the mystery man's lips were moving, shaping the same few words over and over. I gasped and stumbled backward.

"They're all moving!" Mason shouted, pointing at the table.

In every photograph, the man's mouth worked furiously, desperately. We stood helpless, paralyzed with fear, watching until his movements slowed and finally stilled.

Fox kept staring, his breathing rough. I pulled my sweatshirt sleeves down over my hands to slow the cold creeping into my limbs. Mason curled up against me. I could feel his heart racing in his chest.

"So," I said, swallowing, my throat bone-dry, "not a trick camera, then?"

"What's happening?" Mason said. "Is it a ghost? What does he want?"

Fox widened his eyes at me, then tilted his head at Mason. His standard you're-older-you-handle-it look. But the wide eyes remained, seeking reassurance I wasn't sure I could give.

"Don't worry," I said, squeezing Mason's shoulders. "What would a ghost want with us? Nothing, that's what, because there's no such thing. There has to be an explanation. We just need some time to figure this out."

Mason's forehead scrunched. His mouth was shaped to form another question when Fox came to the rescue. He picked up the leather case and held it close to his face, examining the lining inch by inch. "Check this out," he said, tilting the case to show us the clue he'd uncovered: the initials *JG* inked in red on the white silk lining.

"*JG*? Does that help us?" I said.

"We can find out who this is—who owned the camera before now."

I frowned. "How do we know JG is a person? Maybe it means 'joke gift.'" *Or "joyless ghost,"* I thought without meaning to.

Mason wriggled away from me. "Why don't you ask Dad?" he said. "If it is a person, he just sold all their stuff, didn't he?"

Fox nodded. "Best idea of the day," he said. "Josie and I will talk to him. But listen, kiddo. All of this needs to stay a secret for a while, okay?" He pulled a Snickers bar from his pocket and held it out to Mason. "The mystery man, the photos—all of it. Just until we figure out what's making the camera work that way. You know how Dad worries. We don't want him to take it away or anything. Deal?"

Mason grabbed the candy, head bobbing.

"Now, go on and eat that in your room while we finish up here," Fox said.

Mason took off toward the house, already chewing.

I blocked Fox's path, hands on hips. "You still think the camera is rigged? You saw the guy's face, saw his mouth moving. How do you explain that?"

Fox gathered the photos, tucked the camera in its case, and swung the strap over his shoulder. "I can't."

"And you're not even a little bit worried about all this."

"Who, me?" He smiled his most reassuring smile: cocky, unflinching, all pearly whites and lofty eyebrows.

Which set me worrying even more, because it was the smile he used whenever he was lying through his teeth.

3

O N THE WAY BACK TO THE AUCTION HOUSE, we passed a few straggling customers in the lot trying to wedge boxes and lamps and the odd piece of furniture into their cars. Inside, we found Dad sweeping up dried mud from the auction floor. Uncle Bill was stacking chairs. Aunt Barb stood chatting with a neighbor, her own broom long forgotten.

Dad spotted the camera right away. "I should have known that woman was in cahoots with the two of you," he said by way of greeting. "You wasted sixty dollars on that? We must have a dozen old cameras stashed around the house."

"I knew it," Fox muttered. "Pure profit."

"We like this one," I said to drown him out. "It has character."

"Come to think of it," Dad said, scratching his head, "I thought that camera belonged with next week's lot. You kids didn't get that out of the storeroom, did you?"

"'Course not. It was on Table Six with everything

else," Fox said. "It didn't belong to the estate you sold today?"

"No. Maybe Bill mixed it in by accident."

"Whose is it, then?" I said. "We don't even know which estate you have lined up next week."

Dad's mouth quirked upward. "That doesn't sound like my kids, forgetting to make everybody else's business their own."

"And you haven't made us help with inventory or research or any of our usual jobs," Fox countered. "What's the big secret?"

"No secret." Dad clutched his broom a little tighter. "Just been busy. It's a big estate."

"So whose is it?" Fox pressed.

"Just a widower over near Clark." He and his broom skulked away to a section of floor he'd already swept. Fox and I raised our eyebrows at each other.

Clark. A town twenty miles west with its own terrible history. Long story short, most of it was destroyed in a landslide when Dad was a kid. Hundreds dead, buildings unreachable. A whole town, gone. People still talked about it like it'd just happened. The whole thing made my chest feel heavy and cold, as if I couldn't get a decent breath. Of course Fox and I had always, always wanted to go there and see it for ourselves, and of course no one would ever let us.

Fox wasn't giving up on the issue just yet. "A big estate near Clark, huh? It wasn't old Mr. Goodrich, was it?"

Dad rubbed the back of his neck with one hand. He wouldn't look at us.

"Seriously?" I said.

"I can't believe you didn't tell us!" Fox cried. "We almost missed the auction of the century!"

Sighing, Dad set his broom against the wall. "I was going to tell you." He sighed again when he saw our eyes, wide and unblinking. "Come with me."

Haunted camera or no, our interest had just jumped to the moon and back. We followed at his heels as he led us to the storage room that we used for sorting, cataloging, and photographing merchandise.

Dad unlocked the door and pocketed his keys. He threw the master switch to flood the room with light from the double-high ceiling.

Every free inch of space was occupied with second-hand swag.

"This is the Goodrich estate," Dad said.

"Dang," I said.

Our voices sounded hushed and harsh, swallowed up by all the stuff.

Fox couldn't speak. He *always* had something to say, but right then, all he could do was drool. He was probably imagining the money he could make selling just two or three items from the infamous Goodrich estate—even a used toothbrush or a can of motor oil.

Because everyone knew that the Goodrich mansion was one of the few buildings to escape the landslide.

Mrs. Goodrich had been running some sort of errand in town when the landslide hit. They never found her. Mr. Goodrich had been at home and survived, house untouched, the wall of dirt and debris rumbling to a standstill just shy of their property. He pretty much stayed in that house for the next forty years, refusing to leave or relocate. He paid people to bring groceries and keep up the grounds, but basically his life ended along with all those other unlucky people in the disaster.

"Why all the secrecy, Dad?" I wondered, even though I could guess at the answer. Dad was no fool. He knew that if *we* knew he'd landed the Goodrich estate, we would have been hard-pressed to keep our mouths shut.

Dad pushed his hat back to scratch his forehead. "Didn't seem respectful, after what that poor man went through, to turn this place into a circus over it. They even kept his obituary out of the paper until I could get the house cleared out. I've hired a guard up there so people stay off the property, but it won't stay a secret for much longer. Customers are already pestering me about why I haven't advertised next week's auction. The obituary comes out tomorrow." He chuckled. "I'm surprised your aunt hasn't burst from not being able to gossip about it."

"There are initials in the camera case," Fox said. "JG."

"John Goodrich," Dad said quietly. "I hadn't thought about that place in years. I sure never figured I'd be the one to sell off his estate."

I closed my hand around Dad's callused fingers. "What do you remember about the landslide?"

"I was about six—younger than Mason. We'd had a lot of rain, for weeks and weeks. We joked about building an ark. People on TV were starting to talk about the danger of landslides. Then one afternoon we turned on the news and saw that Clark was all but gone. In a town of five hundred people, almost three hundred were killed.

"Goodrich must have been in his forties then. He never had children. Other survivors settled down in surrounding towns, but John Goodrich wouldn't leave. All kinds of stories grew about him—that he'd gone crazy, that his house was haunted by the ghosts of the townspeople."

I nodded along, thinking of at least a dozen other tales kids still told about him at school.

Dad's voice dropped to a near-whisper. "A few weeks ago, Mr. Goodrich asked me to come and see him, to talk about his final wishes. He was very sick; he died just two days later. When I first stepped into that house, it was like going back in time. There were no computers, no flat-screen TVs—no evidence at all he'd even been outside in the last forty years."

I watched Fox trying desperately to keep his focus on Dad, but his eyes kept straying to the room full of waiting treasures. I was curious, too—burning with it, in fact—but trying not to let it show.

Dad noticed anyway. He gestured to the room. "Go on and have a look around. You see something you can't live without, let me know."

"Really?" I blurted, surprised at the change in protocol.

"John's lawyer gave me the option to keep some pieces as partial payment; the profits from the auction are earmarked for a local charity. But be respectful. I'm asking you to keep this to yourselves until I decide when and how to announce the sale and the name of the deceased. Are we clear?"

We nodded.

"I'll leave you to it, then."

I gave his hand a final squeeze before letting go. He smiled and kissed the top of my head, then ambled back out to the auction floor.

I didn't know where to look first. Larger pieces

crowded the fringes of the room: hand-carved furniture, Persian rugs, brass lamps, brooding portraits in gilded frames, silver candelabras, and velvet chairs. Tables held the smaller bits and pieces of the Goodriches' lives: mountains of books, wooden pipes, car parts, watches, photographs, five sets of golf clubs, record albums, musty clothes, stacks of old newspapers and magazines, old TVs and radios, and hundreds of tools. The storeroom was almost always full of stuff, but I'd never seen it so truly *packed* from one end to the other.

Fox had already wandered farther in. I hoped he remembered we were here for information, not to add to his personal collection. Fox collected anything he deemed cool or valuable, or both. His room was filled with old maps and globes, tin toys, printer's blocks, and sports memorabilia. It was like a shrine of auction leftovers, a monument to all his best finds.

And don't get me started on the rest of our house. Momma was a pack rat her whole life, and when Aunt Barb moved in, we found out that she was even worse. Aunt Barb was famous for the phrase "That's a perfectly good (fill in the blank)." Like, "That's a perfectly good piece of used tinfoil," or "That's a perfectly good headless Barbie doll."

I made sure my room was just the opposite. Our family saw firsthand all the stuff people collected over a lifetime, only to have it sold to the highest bidder once they were gone. I didn't see the point. I didn't want piles of belongings for people to fight over when it was my time to go.

Jewelry was my one exception. Momma left me her grandmother's cameo brooch, a pretty piece carved in coral and ox bone. I wore it on a chain around my neck. I'd been hooked on vintage jewelry ever since, and it was the first thing to grab my attention in the storeroom. I lingered over a tray of cocktail rings, admiring a setting done in onyx and marcasite.

As I slipped the ring on my finger, my eye settled on something farther down the table, a glimpse of antennae and pincers and shiny black shells. I stepped closer. It was a grouping of black-framed shadow boxes, each one containing a collection of pinned bugs—beetles, butterflies—and one with all different sizes and shapes of moths. "Yuck," I whispered at the sight of the spindly legs and brittle bodies. My stomach turned. My skin prickled as if I had ants scurrying up and down my arms. Still, I couldn't seem to look away. I reached out, cautious, my hand not quite steady, fingers poised to pick one up.

"Josie?" Fox said inches from my ear, and I nearly jumped out of my skin. My fingers bumped the stacked shadow boxes and sent them skidding off the table.

I grabbed at them to keep them from clattering to the floor.

Fox stood beside me with an open photo album in his hands, his mouth a tight line. "It's him. John Goodrich."

Sure enough, there stood our mystery man. He was much younger, dressed in a tuxedo and standing next to a woman in a wedding dress, but it was definitely him. I took the album and flipped through it page by page. The man appeared in different clothing and different places, always looking pleasant enough, even smiling sometimes. But toward the end, as the styles hit full-on leisure suits, double-wide ties, and sideburns, his expression grew more serious, his eyes more solemn, until, in the very last photo, he looked just the same as he did in our Polaroids, right down to the identical suit and tie.

I clutched the album tighter. I had pretended for Mason's sake that we couldn't possibly be dealing with a ghost. But a knot of worry had settled in my chest, and I could still see fear in Fox's eyes. We both knew the truth, but it seemed easier to keep pretending. I cleared my throat. "So, this picture must be the one he used to rig the camera somehow," I said. "Why would he do it? He doesn't seem like the practical-joker type."

Fox reached out and plucked the picture from the album. He flipped it over and found something written on the back. "It's dated April 18, 1975. The day before the landslide."

"The day before his wife died," I said.

I suddenly felt guilty for poking through this man's belongings. But I swallowed the guilt, handed the album back, and went back to searching. There had to be an answer, a reason Goodrich was haunting those Polaroids.

Fox took one half of the room; I took the other. I wandered up and down the rows, gathering a box of promising items for later inspection.

When we were finished, I had two photo albums, five handwritten journals, and the marcasite ring—because it was pretty and because I knew I could talk Dad into letting me keep it. Fox chose a bundle of maps and papers, a scrapbook of newspaper clippings, and another Polaroid camera about a decade older than the one we'd bought. He'd also picked up a clunky clock radio for Mason to dismantle, knowing Dad would approve. Giving the kid old radios and computer parts kept our curious little brother from taking apart anything valuable.

Dad reappeared, clothes rumpled and dusty from the busy morning. "You about done in here?"

We nodded, trying not to draw attention to our odd array of keepsakes, but Dad's sharp eyes raked over every last item. "You want their old letters and papers? Are you really that curious about these folks?"

We nodded again.

"I'm not sure I'm comfortable with my kids poking around in these people's business. Didn't you find anything else you wanted?" I held out my hand, the ring nestled in my palm. Fox displayed the camera and clock radio. Still, Dad hesitated. "You will not sell these. You will not share them with your friends. I want your word now. These were real people who suffered a real tragedy. I trust you to do the right thing."

"We promise."

"Let's go, then, so I can lock up. You two are the oddest ducks I've ever met." We clutched our treasures tighter in case he changed his mind.

"What will happen to the house?" Fox said.

"The lawyer has asked me to auction that as well. I have to go over there this week to clear out a few last items, have an inspector look at the property—the usual." He saw our faces light up and stopped us in a hurry. "And no, you may not come with me. I think I've been generous enough for one day."

"Yes, Dad," we said, knowing full well that within the hour we'd start pleading our case to go with him. Sure enough, as soon as Dad walked away, Fox turned to me with fire in his eyes. "We're going." And I knew, because Fox had set his mind to it, that it would be so.

* * *

Before we could regroup at the Cave with our finds, Aunt Barb found me and gave me a mountain of laundry to fold, and then I had to help with dinner.

Officially, Aunt Barb and Uncle Bill were living in the apartment above the garage just until we got back on our feet after Momma died. Unofficially, they made sure the bills got paid and the family got fed and all those other pesky details that sometimes slipped Dad's mind.

I had no intention of letting them leave, ever.

Aunt Barb fit right into the Fletcher family. Like Momma, she was loud with a capital L. She laughed loud; she talked loud. Her clothes were loud. She and Momma both had wild red hair that curled any which way it pleased. They always used to love bickering about who was the better cook. And next to our mom, Aunt Barb was the kindest, funniest lady in all of Athens County.

Any other night Fox and I would be savoring every last bite of her blue-ribbon cooking. But that night we had bigger fish to fry. While we concentrated on inhaling our food as quickly as possible, Mason kept staring at Fox and me from across the table. His sneakers thumped against the chair legs as he ate, a sure sign that the day had been too much, too exciting and full, and he was ready to burst from it all. But other than spilling his milk and showing us mouthfuls of chewed food just for the shock value, he kept his wits enough not to bring up the camera or any of the day's strange events.

Dad gave us a few odd looks, too. I tried to smile innocently around bites of chicken lasagna. Uncle Bill said very little, as usual, so Aunt Barb filled the silence with the latest town gossip she'd traded that morning, like how Sue Ann what's-her-name had some "work done" and how long Abe Simmons had been out of a job and whether anyone would ever hire such a layabout anyhow.

Fox had dish duty that night. I told him to meet me in my room when he was done, glad for the chance to be alone with my tangled thoughts. Mason ran off to "fix" the radio Fox had scrounged for him.

I fanned the Goodrich albums and journals out on the bed, then sat down in the middle of them and opened a photo album with *John + Nora* embossed in gold on the front cover. I lingered over photographs of them standing on the Great Wall of China, kissing in front of the Eiffel Tower, and walking hand in hand along a white-sand beach. They looked happy and normal.

So they loved to travel. They had a ton of money. They probably could have lived anywhere they wanted.

Why stay in Clark, Ohio? I set the album aside and reached for one of the journals.

The first one looked like a record of financial transactions. Columns and columns of numbers filled the pages, organized by month and year and sprinkled with words like *net*, *gross*, *profit/loss*, and *interest accrued*. By page three, I'd nearly gone cross-eyed from boredom. Impatient, I skimmed the second book and found it was more of the same.

I made myself read every page, but the figures were starting to blur by the time Fox knocked and opened the door a crack to peek in. "Josie? What are you doing?"

I nodded at the journal in my hand.

"Anything interesting?" he said as he entered, his arms full of maps and papers.

"Just financial stuff so far."

He held up the scrapbook of newspaper clippings he'd found. "Check this out. There are a handful of articles about the landslide, but the rest are about other disasters, most of them in Ohio and West Virginia." He set the open book on the bed. I shivered as I paged through it and saw what he meant. Headlines shouted up at me, describing car crashes and train derailments, freak storms and fires.

"About half of them are dated before the landslide," Fox said. "The rest are after. Talk about a creepy hobby."

Half-formed ideas spilled out as I tried to work through what we knew. "So a man obsessed with disasters survives a horrible landslide that wiped out his whole town. Instead of moving away, he stays there for forty years, surrounded by reminders of the tragedy every single day. That doesn't sound like someone trying to forget." I pointed at the scrapbook. "He collected articles about it. That's so messed up. Do you think . . . Is there any chance . . . ?"

"You think he had something to do with the landslide?" Fox said. "How? Why? His wife died, Josie."

"I know. It's just such a crazy coincidence. Did you find anything else?"

He lifted the stack of papers and maps he'd claimed from the storeroom. "We still have all these to go through."

I sighed. Research wasn't as exciting as I'd expected, and it had been too long of a day to sift through endless papers in search of clues that might not even exist.

I really did want to know who John Goodrich was, why he'd fallen into our lives this way. But I also worried that the more we learned, the more we wouldn't like what we found.

"Oh, I also checked out that other camera," Fox said.

"And?"

He answered by taking a stack of Polaroids from

his pile of research and tossing them at me. "See for yourself."

"You're kidding." There were photos of his bedroom, the kitchen, the hallway, the backyard. Our friend Mr. Goodrich stared, sad-eyed, from every last one of them. "These are all from the *second* camera?"

"Uh-huh."

"This is nuts." Suddenly I felt wrung out. My head ached. My eyes were gritty and sore. I needed normal for a little while.

I shooed Fox out, confident he would spend hours poring over his pile of research and fill me in on any new developments when he was ready. I changed into my pink plaid pajamas and went downstairs to watch TV. Dad was already watching a basketball game, so I snuggled up next to him on the couch, trying to cheer in all the right places. Aunt Barb was on the phone with some person who somehow hadn't heard about Sue Ann what's-her-name. Leaning farther into the curve of Dad's shoulder, I let the sound of Aunt Barb's voice wash over me. She sounded so much like Momma it made my heart squeeze. But I felt lucky, too, glad to have my family right there close.

When I felt myself nodding off around nine o'clock, I said good-night and went up to bed, trying not to think about our unsettling day. I kissed the framed picture of

Momma on my bedside table. I heard Mason still awake, arguing for a later bedtime, Aunt Barb starting a load of laundry, Dad making something in the microwave. Slowly, the noises faded and the house fell quiet, but I couldn't fall asleep. My thoughts kept circling back to John Goodrich staring out of those photographs, lips moving—like he was trying to get our attention.

I wished I hadn't stashed the Polaroids in my bedroom. Their presence felt like a pebble in a shoe, a black smudge on my tidy room. I curled up under the blankets, trying to make myself as small as possible, but the presence only grew, thick and heavy and impossible to ignore.

The house creaked and thumped as it settled for the night. Branches scraped the window. A dog barked somewhere far away. Our old furnace rumbled to life with a throaty cough. I peeked out of the covers just as two red pinpoints flared to life beyond the curtains.

I sat up with a gasp. A dark form moved past the glass, followed by a sound like flapping wings.

Then the lights, and the figure, were gone.

It was a barn owl. Had to be. An owl, or hawk, or— what other creatures liked to stay awake at night? It didn't matter, because it was no big deal. Just some bird out looking for its dinner. Or maybe a bat. Didn't bats have red eyes? I could look it up. Yes, definitely a bat. I

crept to the end of the bed and pressed my nose to the glass, my quick breaths fogging the window. But there was nothing there.

I lay there for another hour, pulse thrumming, before sinking into exhausted sleep, dreaming of a thousand red eyes flung like stars across the walls and ceiling of my room.

4

SUNDAY DAWNED CLEAR AND COLD. OUTSIDE
my window, a layer of frost blanketed the fields
and rooftops, shining in the morning sunlight. I sat up,
kissed the photo of Momma, and sank my bare toes into
the fluffy rug beside my bed.

I felt a prickle between my shoulder blades, a rising
sense of being watched by unseen eyes. I glanced at the
closet door. Maybe Fox would keep the photos in his
room for a few days. But I was too chicken to ask him.
Practical, predictable Josie, afraid of a few photographs?
I'd never hear the end of it.

"Josie, you awake?" Fox waltzed in without waiting
for an answer. "Guess what? I found a few very interesting items in that pile of papers."

I stood and stretched. "Like what?" I said, still fighting
the urge to look over my shoulder.

"I found surveyors' maps and aerial photos of Clark.
And there were minutes from town meetings where Goodrich and his wife showed up to rant about landslides,

trying to get an evacuation plan put in place or hire people to assess the danger," Fox said. "They were trying to warn people about the disaster months before it happened."

"How would they know about the landslide unless they had something to do with it?" I said.

"But why would they warn people if they did it on purpose?"

Good question.

"And get this," he continued. "It wasn't just landslides. They donated all this money to buy fancy weather equipment, enforce stricter building codes, install more traffic signals, build a new fire station, add a wing to the town medical center. We're talking millions of dollars."

I ran my hands through my tangled hair. Fox was already showered and dressed in khakis and a sweater-vest, an outfit that would turn most kids into instant bully magnets. But Fox wasn't most kids. He looked like an escapee from a young-executive training program. "How long have you been up?" I said.

"Long enough."

"But how—"

"Look, we'll talk about it on the way. Just get dressed. Dad's going to Clark *today*."

"What?"

"I'm pretty sure he plans to go this morning to avoid us trying to tag along."

"Smart man."

Fox and I were sitting in Dad's truck by the time he came outside. He saw us and stopped short. We smiled and waved.

He swung the driver's side door open and slid behind the wheel. "Just going out for doughnuts," Dad said. "No need for you two to come along. I'll bring back your favorites, all right?"

"We're old enough," Fox countered, arms crossed. "Why can't we come?"

"For doughnuts?"

"To Clark," Fox said. "You already let us go through their stuff, encouraged our thirst for knowledge. You can't cut us off now when we're learning so much about our community's tragic history."

Dad narrowed his eyes, calling bull on Fox's little speech.

So Fox resorted to a primitive but effective method of persuasion to speed things along. "Pleeeeaaase?"

I joined in. "Please, Dad?"

"Get your seat belts on," Dad grumbled, blowing into his cold-stiffened hands. "Does your aunt know you're leaving?"

Fox grinned. "I left her a note."

Dad was a man of his word. He stopped for doughnuts on the way out of town.

During the drive to Clark, Fox and I played Last Doughnut Standing, a time-honored game of eating as slowly as possible to see who could make their doughnut last the longest.

"You mind telling me what you two are hoping to find out here?" Dad said.

"Come on, Dad, everybody's interested in this place," Fox said, chewing a microscopic bite of his cruller. "How could we turn down a chance to see inside? Besides, isn't there a good chance that whoever buys it at auction will have it bulldozed?"

He nodded. "That's right. There's already talk of a memorial being built on the site."

The hills were a menacing presence as we drove, higher and steeper than in Athens. As I ate my sprinkles one at a time, I tried to imagine what it must have been like for John Goodrich and his wife. Fox had said they tried to warn the town. Had they really known about the landslide? How could anyone have known? I pictured Goodrich sitting calmly in his study, maybe drinking coffee or reading a book. Maybe he heard a noise—a low rumble at first, growing until it rattled the windows, until it deafened him. He must have looked outside to see half the mountain sliding toward him—

I startled when the truck's motion changed as Dad

slowed and took the exit for Clark. I sat up taller, craning my neck for a glimpse of the ruined town. Finally, we rounded a bend in the road.

The hillside looked . . . liquefied. A river of rock and dirt flowed from hilltop to valley, much of it covered by a newer growth of brush and scrub trees.

We passed structures here and there along the road, long abandoned: the boarded-up brick school, the bare bones of an old gas station, a rusted playground. I pressed my face close to the window. All that remained of the playground were a set of monkey bars and one lonely swing, swaying in the breeze. Weeds and tall grasses had swallowed the rest.

A rush of dread filled me. I nearly insisted that Dad take us home. But Fox's face shone with anticipation. Dad gripped the steering wheel loosely, looking relaxed. The only one fool enough to feel nervous was me.

Dad turned the truck down a narrow, rutted road, and suddenly I was staring at the Goodrich house for the first time.

I'd always imagined it as a gloomy clapboard farmhouse with a sagging porch, a weather vane, and jagged holes in the roof. But the real thing was more unsettling than anything I'd invented in my head.

The house had probably been beautiful once, with

thick wooden beams in angled patterns around the windows and a roof shaped by sharp peaks and valleys. But decades of neglect had left it scarred, layers of moss and black grime clinging to every surface. Tall, thin trees lined the driveway, their branches shivering in the wind.

Dad parked the truck and we scrambled out. A man I didn't recognize rose from a chair on the porch and approached to shake Dad's hand. Pale and blond with a baby face, he kind of looked like a kid and a grown-up all at the same time.

He was also over six feet tall and built like a pro wrestler.

"Mitch, I'd like you to meet my two oldest kids, Fox and Josie." Fox shook the man's hand. I hesitated, a little afraid that he'd squash my fingers, but eventually I held out my hand.

Mitch took it in both of his own. His grip was strong but not crushing. "Pleased to make your acquaintance, Josie. That's a solid handshake you have there." His gentle, soft-spoken voice was completely at odds with his mammoth size.

"Any problems out here?" Dad asked.

"No, sir." He gestured to the pair of earbuds he wore, the cord disappearing into his coat pocket. "Had to bring along some music to drown out the quiet. It gets to you after a while."

Dad nodded. "The kids and I came to gather the last few items for auction. And I'm meeting the inspector at ten. Will you give us a heads-up when he gets here?"

"Sure thing, Mr. Fletcher."

We climbed the porch steps, and Dad unlocked the front door and led us inside. Our movements echoed through the empty space.

We stood in the center of a two-story great room. Underfoot, the scuffed wooden floors creaked and groaned. The ceiling soared overhead. Paneled walls and wooden beams made the room feel too dark, especially since the windows were shrouded by thick velvet curtains.

I walked over to yank the curtains aside, letting light flood the room. A thick chill hung in the air, creeping into my bones. I lingered at the window to let the sun warm my face, until I caught a clear view of the ruined mountain.

I quickly closed the drapes again.

I heard Fox and Dad climbing a set of stairs; soon their footsteps thumped overhead, their murmured voices drifting down through the ceiling. In the dining room, I passed three Persian rugs, rolled up and propped in a corner, and a handful of sealed boxes. I stepped into the kitchen. The oven was big enough to use in a restaurant, though outdated by several decades. Over the sink, a large picture window faced the mountain—another reminder of the disaster. Had John been at the window? Had he seen it coming?

I moved through an arched doorway, past a marble fireplace, and ran my hand along the smooth wooden banister that led up to the second floor.

Fox stood at the top of the stairs. "Is there a basement?" he said as he came down.

"Not sure. Where's Dad?"

"In the master bedroom. There's a safe in the wall up there. He's trying to work his magic. Couldn't crack it the last time he was out here. Says he might have to bring in Lucky Larry from town."

"It's a pretty house," I said, wandering back toward the windows. "Not what I pictured at all." I fingered a section of peeling wallpaper. "But all that sadness and death . . . it feels like it's soaked right into the walls, you know?" My voice sounded dreamy, far away to my own ears.

Fox followed me and snapped his fingers in front of my face. "Josie, you in there? What's going on with you?"

I shoved his hand away. "Nothing. Everything! How can you not feel—"

A shout of terror came from upstairs, our father's voice in a tone I'd never heard, and then, even as we went running, a terrible series of thumps and thuds and grunts of pain.

We found Dad sprawled at the bottom of the stairs, eyelids fluttering, one hand opening and closing uselessly, his right leg twisted the wrong way beneath him.

"Daddy!" I stood stupidly, gaping, the scene so awful I couldn't move.

"Josie, get Mitch. Now!" Fox shook my shoulders and gave me a push toward the front door before kneeling and grabbing Dad's hand to still his fingers. I ran, shouting for Mitch. He barreled through the door, already punching numbers into his cell phone. Fox had started up a stream of calming chatter, pushing gently on Dad's shoulder each time he tried to get up off the floor. Fox had taken off his coat and draped it over Dad's chest. I moved to do the same, but Mitch beat me to it. I nearly sobbed in gratitude because I was suddenly so cold I couldn't catch my breath. My teeth chattered. As I leaned in close, I could hear Dad's distressed muttering, the same few words again and again: "Red eyes. He flew right at me with those red, red eyes."

My gaze flew to Fox. I hadn't told anyone about the red eyes outside my window. What could it mean? But now wasn't the time to ask, especially when I saw Fox's impassive face. His eyes were shuttered, his body statue-still. In the years since we lost Momma, it had become his default setting anytime fear tapped him on the shoulder. He caught me staring and looked away.

Mitch, phone to his ear, squeezed my arm with one huge hand. I flinched.

Sirens wailed. People came and bundled Dad up and hustled him into an ambulance. Mitch made several calls—to Uncle Bill and Aunt Barb, to the inspector and the Goodrich lawyer. Fox helped, kept himself busy, seemed in his element organizing and making things happen.

I huddled in a corner with Mitch's coat over me,

trying to stay out of the way, trying to process what had happened.

Mitch said unsettling things into the phone: fractured leg, shock, likely concussion. When I was little, I used to think it would be great to break a bone so you wouldn't have to go to school. Everyone would bring you presents and feel bad for you and sign your cast.

Then, when I was eight, I broke my collarbone. I missed the school Halloween party *and* trick-or-treating. I had to wear a weird brace thing under my clothes, so no one could even sign it; it just made me look lumpy. The pain kept me awake at night, and when I felt bad for bothering my parents again and again, I just lay there and cried.

I wondered if it was the same for grown-ups. Would Dad cry if the pain got too bad, if there was no one around to see? He cried at Momma's funeral, but that was a different kind of hurt. After three years, it had become a sort of distant ache, but every once in a while it flared back up, fierce and blinding, like a broken bone. For Mason and me, a good cry usually helped us ride out the worst of it, but Dad and Fox preferred working, planning, problem solving—anything to deflect that staggering pain.

Eventually, Fox came and sat down beside me.

"You okay?" I said, hoping to regain some credibility as the big sister.

He swallowed. "Yeah. You?"

"I guess so. Hey, Fox?"

"Yeah?"

"Last night I saw red eyes outside my window." I kept my voice low so Mitch wouldn't overhear. "I thought maybe it was a bird or a bat or something. But now I'm not so sure."

Fox stared at me.

"And just now, Dad said he saw . . . "

"I know," Fox said. "I heard."

I took a deep breath. One of us had to come out and say it. "Okay, so for starters, we have the ghost of John Goodrich popping up in those photographs. Agreed?"

He nodded.

"And Dad and I saw red eyes in two different places. One of them *indoors*."

Another nod.

I spotted a dead fly curled up against the baseboard near my feet. An impossible, terrifying idea teased at the edge of my thoughts.

"So you think they're related?" he prompted.

I didn't answer right away. Like most kids in Athens, we wore our ghostly reputation as a badge of honor. We scared each other silly trying to top the whoppers the last kid told about whispers in the woods or an angry spirit in the rafters. But I could think of only one local legend with red eyes: Mothman.

Mothman was the triple threat of scary stories: real eyewitnesses, a grotesque inhuman creature, and a bona fide disaster where people lost their lives. Forty-six victims died that awful day nearly fifty years ago, their cars plunging into the Ohio River when the Silver Bridge gave way. In the months leading up to the disaster, witnesses around town were menaced by a strange creature—part man, part moth. No one knew for sure whether Mothman caused the collapse or tried to warn people away, but either way he was nothing to take lightly.

"Josie? What is it?"

"Dad said 'he.' *He* flew right at me with those red, red eyes.'"

"So?"

"So who do you know of around here that flies and has red eyes?"

I saw the moment he understood. "Mothman?" he said. "The thing from Point Pleasant?"

"Why not?" I said, forgetting to whisper.

"What does he have to do with anything?"

"How am I supposed to know?"

Mitch glanced over at the sound of our raised voices. I pressed my lips together and offered a halfhearted wave until he turned away again.

Fox leaned in and muttered, "I'm still having a hard

time with the whole ghost thing, okay? Now we're gonna throw Mothman into the mix?"

"I didn't throw him in there."

"You brought him up." He crossed his arms, as if he considered the matter closed.

I sighed.

We stared at nothing for a while.

"Do you think Dad ever got the safe open?" Fox asked.

I blinked. "I'm not sure."

He glanced at Mitch, who was still making calls, then glided up the stairs. I stood at the bottom and waited. Fox didn't have to go farther than the landing at the top. He knelt and started gathering something— papers, it looked like. "Josie, come and help me," he whisper-called.

I crept up the stairs one at a time, wondering if those red eyes were still in the house somewhere.

"Faster," he hissed.

I made it to the top and found that Dad had spilled a shoe box full of papers. Fox was shoveling them back into the box as fast as he could scoop them up. "These must be from the safe. Help me make sure I don't miss anything."

I knelt and started feeling around the dingy carpet. My hand skimmed something sharp, and a glint of gold caught my eye. It was an old-fashioned stickpin. Worried

Fox might try to claim it for himself, I slipped it into my pocket before he could see.

"Kids?" Mitch called.

"Coming!" Fox said. "Just getting Dad's things for him."

We met Mitch at the bottom of the stairs.

"Come on, I'll take you home," Mitch said. He eyed the shoe box. "You find something up there?"

"Just some of my dad's papers," Fox said.

Mitch reached for the box. "Why don't you let me hang on to those for you? Just until your dad gets home."

Fox clung to the box. "That's okay. I've got it."

"Can't we go to the hospital to see Dad?" I asked.

"He might be in surgery for a little while. Your family will bring you over when they say it's okay."

"Surgery?" I said. My heart stuttered. "But he just broke his leg."

"Looked like a bad break. Sometimes they have to put pins in to keep it stable."

He sounded so matter-of-fact, but what did he know? Dad could have died on the way to the hospital. He could die during surgery. On TV there were always "complications." *We should have gone with him to the hospital*, I thought. *We should be with him, not here with some stranger. Why are they acting so calm?* Fox seemed more worried about his box of papers than he was about Dad. I glared at the both of them, shoved Mitch's coat at him, and stormed outside. Was it still morning? I felt as if a hundred years had passed.

I knew from when we lost Momma that sometimes *scared* and *angry* got tangled up with each other. I tried not to let the anger win out, but I couldn't seem to shut it off. We'd already had more than our share of heartache. It wasn't fair.

I stopped short in the driveway, unsure if we were taking Dad's truck or Mitch's much older compact.

"We'll take my car," Mitch said. "Your uncle said he would come for the truck later on."

It hit me that Mitch considered this an accident, something unlucky but easily explained. Fresh resentment flared. How could he not see that something terrible was taking hold of our family?

UNCLE BILL HAD ALREADY LEFT FOR THE
hospital by the time we made it home. Mason
met us at the front door, eyes fearful. I hugged him close
and told him not to worry, but still he looked to Fox for
reassurance. Fox handed me the box of papers from the
safe, then hustled Mason off to play video games, shrug-
ging an apology at me. Aunt Barb tried to fuss over me,
but I just wanted to be alone. I locked myself in my room
and took out the pin I'd found.

It was a woman's stickpin, 14 karat gold. I'd seen similar pins that were a hundred years old or more. But
what caught my attention was the fact that the face of
the pin, no bigger than a dime, contained a preserved
moth under glass.

I held the pin close to my face and breathed on it to
fog the glass. I wiped it clean on my shirt, then held it in
my palm and stared at it. You could still see the moth's
tiny antennae, its furry body, the veins in its paper-thin
wings. What kind of person would own such a spooky

piece of jewelry on purpose? I turned it over and over, examining every inch, mesmerized.

Finally I put the pin aside and started paging through the journals from the storeroom. They were as boring as ever. My thoughts kept wandering back to Dad, hurt and alone at the hospital except for introverted Uncle Bill. Still, I kept at it until the light outside my window dimmed. The sun was going down. My stomach rumbled and I realized I'd missed lunch. Had there been any news? Why hadn't Aunt Barb been up to let me know? I let myself picture the worst outcome possible. My heart clenched, missing Momma for the millionth time, and now Dad, too.

I placed the pin in my lockbox, squared my shoulders, and went downstairs. Aunt Barb was stirring something on the stove. It smelled amazing.

"Hi, honey. You okay?"

She wouldn't be cooking if something had happened to Dad, would she? I was almost too afraid to ask. "Any news?"

"Your dad's surgery went just fine. He's resting tonight. Tomorrow I'll take you all over to see him."

I felt light-headed with relief. "That's great. Wow, okay. That's really great."

"I tried knocking on your door earlier to tell you, but you didn't answer. I thought maybe you fell asleep."

"Oh." I didn't remember anyone knocking.

"Anyhow, potato soup for dinner. Tell the boys to wash up, okay?"

"Sure."

"Josie, you sure you're all right? You look awfully pale."

"Yeah. It's just been a really bad day."

I let her wrap me in a hug, suddenly more grateful for the attention than I could say. "Poor little duckling." She clicked her tongue. "Your dad should never have taken you and your brother out there. That whole place is cursed."

I pulled away. "Cursed?"

Her eyes widened. Her lips folded shut. I'd never seen anyone backpedal so quickly. "Well, you know what I mean. With the landslide and everything."

"Who says it's cursed?"

"You know how people talk. It's nothing. Some things are best forgotten."

"Aunt Barb." I pinned her with a pleading look. She couldn't keep a secret to herself to save her own life, and I knew even just a nudge in the right direction would get her talking. "I could use a good story. To take my mind off this morning." Okay, so that made me feel as crummy as a crust of bread, but if she had information we needed, then it had to be done.

"Well, you know about Point Pleasant and the collapsed bridge. How folks saw the flying moth man before the bridge disaster? It was all over the news back then. They even made a movie about it."

Mothman again. I shuddered. "But after Point Pleasant he disappeared, right? The Mothman?"

"Mothman, yes, that's what they called him. And that's what *they* want you to think."

"Who?"

"The government."

Uh-oh. There was a good chance this was less about actual, useful information and more about Aunt Barb's love for conspiracy theories.

She paused to add a few dashes of salt to the soup, then sprinkled some into her hand and tossed it over her shoulder.

"So the government . . . ?" I prompted.

"Oh yes. Mothman appeared in Clark as well, but the government covered it up to keep people from disturbing the site."

My mind filtered furiously, trying to salvage any kernels of truth from what was likely a forty-year-old piece of gossip.

Was it possible? Did people in Clark really see Mothman? Momma and Aunt Barb grew up in northern Kentucky, so the landslide would have been on Aunt Barb's radar. Whether her information was based on memory or hand-me-down rumors was another story.

"Who saw him? How did they cover it up?"

"Hmmm? Oh, I think many of the people who saw him were killed in that terrible landslide. But the stories still got out, thanks to survivors like Eva."

"Who?"

She paused again to dip a spoon into the soup and take a cautious sip. "Mmm. More garlic, I think."

I gritted my teeth to cage my impatience. To women like Aunt Barb, stories were to be savored, like soup, seasoned to perfection, sampled, and stretched out to make them last.

"Eva. My hairdresser. She was a housekeeper for Mr. Goodrich. Worked there some twenty-five years before she was suddenly let go. She's told me a story or two."

I blinked. Someone who'd worked right there in the house? It was like a Christmas present, all done up with a fancy bow. "What did she say about Mothman?"

"Oh, goodness knows if it's true."

"But?"

She paused and studied my face, suddenly aware perhaps of how loose her tongue had become. But I must have passed her test, maybe even got promoted to gossip-in-training. I was almost thirteen, after all.

"Mothman appeared in that very house, more than once."

"Before the landslide, or after?"

"Both. That's the first thing I thought of when I heard about your daddy. Of course that's just stories, just tales passed around." She gave a nervous laugh.

"Right. Of course."

Both, my mind screamed at me.

She shooed me out of the kitchen, conversation over. "Go and get your brothers, now."

Could Mothman really be tied up in all this somehow? *No*, I thought. *No way*. Things were already complicated enough. Aunt Barb loved a good story. She'd heard a juicy piece of gossip about the Goodrich place and couldn't help but pass it on.

It was tough to concentrate on eating after that, but it helped that the soup tasted like heaven itself. I savored the feel of it warming me from the inside, and tried for just those few seconds not to think about any-thing else.

"Do we have to go to school tomorrow?" Mason asked.

"Gracious, I don't know," Aunt Barb said. "I think you could miss a day for the sake of visiting your daddy."

"But when is he coming home?" Mason said.

"In a few days, dumpling."

I could tell by the way he fidgeted in his chair that Fox wanted to talk about the papers from the safe. He'd been stuck playing with Mason all afternoon.

After we cleaned up the kitchen, Aunt Barb sat at the table with Mason making get-well cards for Dad. Fox and I went upstairs.

We got settled on the floor of my room with the box between us and sorted through the papers one by one. There were contracts, receipts, ledgers—even a few cards and letters from John to his wife and vice versa.

About halfway through the box, I found something strange. "Fox, look at this."

It was a piece of lined notebook paper with a series of numbers and the words *SAVE THEM* printed in neat block letters.

"What do you think it means? Is that a safe combina-tion?" I said.

"Hmm. Measurements, maybe? Could be a date. Or a time."

"Could it be an address? Or some kind of code?"

"Truth is, it could be just about anything," Fox said with a shrug.

"I guess you're right." I set the paper aside and kept looking, but it turned out to be the only interesting thing in the box.

"Should we take one more look around the store-room?" I said.

"Yeah, good idea." He rubbed a hand over his face. I realized he actually looked less than his usual pressed and polished self.

We stashed the notebook page in the lockbox and put the rest of the papers in Dad's office. Then we stopped at Mason's room to say good-night. Aunt Barb had already tucked him in, his hair still damp and sweet-smelling from the shower.

He sat up as soon as he saw us. "Where are you going? Does it have anything to do with the g-h-o-s-t?"

I shushed him. "What makes you think we're going anywhere?"

"Because everything exciting happens after I'm in bed."

"We're just going out to the storeroom," Fox said. You're not missing anything. I promise."

"It's not fair. Why do you get to stay up later than me? I want to come, too."

I shook my head. "Not this time."

Mason stuck out his lower lip, watching our faces to see if we changed our minds. When he saw we weren't about to budge, he shrugged, closed his eyes, and said, "Okay. Good night."

Downstairs, we found Aunt Barb sitting on the couch watching TV and knitting. We told her I had lost a ring in the storeroom and we wanted to go look for it. Her brows scrunched together. "It's getting late. And it's awfully chilly out there."

"We won't be long," I promised. "Please? It's my favorite ring. I just have to find it." I tried out a less obvious version of Mason's pout.

Fox jingled Dad's spare keys in his coat pocket.

"Make it quick, then," she said. "And take a flashlight."

Fox held up his other hand. "Done."

In the storeroom, we got right to work digging through dresser drawers and boxes, inside books and between the pages of magazines.

I couldn't say just what we were looking for. As we searched, I casually mentioned Aunt Barb's story placing Mothman at the Goodrich house—just to hear Fox say how crazy it was, how it wasn't worth another thought.

"And you didn't say anything to her about Mothman first?" he asked.

"No. Aunt Barb's the one who brought it up. But it's

just a coincidence. Right? Just a piece of gossip she heard somewhere."

He chewed his lip, a nervous habit he never displayed in public. "Just . . . keep an eye out for anything to do with moths or Mothman," he said. "Just in case."

I remembered the moth shadow box and grabbed it straightaway, even though it still made me squirm. Fox scrounged up an encyclopedia of insects and a book about the disaster in Point Pleasant. I found a few books on the paranormal and two small journals tucked inside a wooden tool chest.

Our time was running short when movement caught the corner of my eye. An old console TV had flickered to life. I looked again to make sure I wasn't seeing things. Sure enough, static filled the screen, growing brighter by the second. I walked over for a closer look and found the power cord dangling out the back.

It wasn't plugged in.

Fox came up beside me, peering at the phantom set through narrowed eyes. We both jumped when a second TV joined the first, this one a portable black-and-white, a writhing square of light in the cavernous room.

Goose bumps crept up my arms. The temperature dropped, as if we'd wandered into a sudden snowstorm.

The static built, rising from an angry hiss to a harsh crush of sound.

Radios switched on one by one, their dials flying back and forth through the stations: the twang of banjos, a swell of opera, a weather report, a thumping hip-hop rhythm, a sportscaster calling the highlights of a basketball game. Sounds mixed and clashed, an agony of noise, pierced by screeches, and moans, and a thousand desperate pleas.

We stood there trembling, cowering, as items lifted from the tables of their own accord, hovering in the air for a few seconds before beginning a slow orbit around the room. The furniture and other oversize pieces fol-

lowed, looming several feet over our heads. My knees buckled. I sprawled on the concrete floor as objects swirled faster and faster around us.

"Save them."

It was a man's voice, low and distorted, amplified all through the space from every radio in the room.

The voice persisted, loud enough to carry over the chaos: "Save them. Save them."

Fox pulled me to my feet. The now-familiar image of John Goodrich stared out from the TVs, drifting above us in the cloud of merchandise. Goodrich repeated only the two words—"Save them"—before the image flickered and started again, a ghostly loop.

I clutched Fox's arm to steady us both. He clutched back, an anchor in a terrifying sea.

Objects swirled faster still. A few flew dangerously close to our heads, so we ducked under the nearest table. The air grew bitterly cold. Our panicked breaths fogged the air. My sobs and Fox's shouts of fear added to the commotion.

"Savethemsavethemsavethemsavethemsavethem."

"Save who?" I screamed back, hands pressed to my ears. "We don't know what you want!"

A light shattered high above, then another and another, glass raining down around us. The room was pitched into blackness. Only the blue-gray light from the televisions remained. Then even that winked out.

Everything went still. We waited. Fox switched on the flashlight and inched his arm out from under the table to shine it around. The room looked normal. Every item was back in its proper place, just as before.

A breath shuddered out of me. Fox sat on the floor, knees drawn up, a death grip on the flashlight. I felt wobbly and weak. I crawled closer to Fox and we sat, gulping down air. The darkness felt alive, like it could reach out with cold, cruel fingers and drag us away.

As the minutes passed, I started to wonder whether Aunt Barb had heard the commotion when high-pitched screams reached our ears, long and panicked, barely pausing for air in between. Not Aunt Barb.

Mason.

We ran, glass crunching beneath our feet, Fox's flashlight bobbing in front of us to point the way.

We barreled outside, across the lawn, through the front door, and up the stairs. We found Mason on the floor of his room, curled in a ball, hands clamped over his ears, screaming. Aunt Barb knelt beside him, hands hovering, but she didn't touch him. The pieces of two dismantled Polaroid cameras lay scattered around him in a messy circle.

I knelt across from Aunt Barb and placed a gentle hand on Mason's shoulder. "Mason. Mason, honey." He jerked away and started up a rocking motion, back and forth, back and forth. I felt like joining him. Instead, I wrapped both arms around him and gathered him into my lap. I rubbed his back, smoothed his hair. "Mason. It's over. We're here. It's over." Of course I had no idea what he'd seen, but I could guess it was something close to our episode in the storeroom. I made soft shushing noises, again and again, until the screams gave way to quiet gasps and sobs.

Aunt Barb looked close to tears, too, her face pale and blank. "I should call your daddy."

"No, it's okay," Fox said. "We don't want to bother him while he's recovering." He nodded at Mason. "Do you know what set him off?"

She wrung her hands, her plump fingers worrying back and forth in nervous circles. "No. I was downstairs when he just started screaming. Has he done this before? Since . . . your momma passed?"

"No," Fox and I said together. Mason had cried plenty of times since Momma died, had even thrown the occasional tantrum, but nothing like this.

We needed some time alone to find out what he'd seen. "Aunt Barb, maybe you could bring him some of your famous hot chocolate?"

"Of course. Mason, I'll be right back, sugar beet."

He sat up as soon as she left, face flushed and splotchy, his breathing jolted by the occasional hiccup, but he stayed nestled in the crook of my arm. "The pieces were floating."

Fox picked up a piece of camera and examined it. "All around the room, right?"

Mason nodded.

"You weren't supposed to touch these."

"I'm sorry. I shouldn't have done it. I just wanted to see what was inside."

"Then what happened?" Fox said.

He sniffed. "I heard a voice from my Batman radio. You told me not to say anything about the man in the pictures, and I thought this might be a secret, too, so I didn't tell Aunt Barb."

Fox ruffled Mason's hair. "You did great, kiddo. Do you remember what the voice said?"

Mason's lower lip jutted out. His eyes filled with new tears.

"The same thing happened to us just now, in the storeroom," I told him. "But nobody got hurt. It was just a lot of noise meant to get our attention, okay?"

"Dad got hurt," he said. Images of Dad at the bottom of those stairs, his leg twisted, flashed through my mind. "That was an accident," I said, mostly to convince myself.

"Save them."

"What?" I said.

"The voice said, 'Save them.' I thought it meant that you were in trouble, that you'd get hurt like Dad did."

"Oh, honey." I was fumbling for something else reassuring to say when a piece of camera—a faceplate—rattled and bounced on the floor. Mason clutched me tighter. All three of us scooted backward.

The camera spit out a photograph. A beat of silence followed. Then the camera rattled and spit out another one, then another. Soon the pictures were coming faster and faster, a small pile quickly building on the carpet with no end in sight. Mason broke free of me and scrambled onto his bed, whimpering. Fox hesitated for only a moment. Then he grabbed Mason's trash can, scooped up all the photos and the pieces of both cameras, and slammed them into the metal can with a satisfying *clunk*. He took the can and left the room, passing Aunt Barb on her way in.

"How are you feeling, sweet potato?" she asked Mason, who stood on his bed, wedged into the corner where two walls met. Cautiously, she held out a mug, the steam rising like Fox's and my breaths had back in the storeroom. Now that Fox had carted off the cameras, Mason started to calm down. I got him to sit cross-legged on the bed. He accepted the mug and took long, careful sips as Aunt Barb sat beside him, looking much calmer herself.

"I think I'll, um . . ." I pointed out the open door. "Get ready for bed?"

Aunt Barb nodded.

"He must have fallen asleep, had a bad dream," I offered. "He's probably worried about Dad."

"I'm sure that's it."

"Okay, then. Good night."

"Night, Josie."

Fox came to the doorway while I was brushing my teeth. "I threw it all out," he told me. "It's in the Dumpster behind the auction building."

"Okay."

"And I locked everything up. The only thing that's noticeable is that all the bulbs blew in the storeroom. Hopefully Uncle Bill will think it was just a power surge."

"What about the shadow box and the books we found?"

"They're still there. I don't want them."

"So that's it? We're done with Goodrich?"

His jaw worked. "He went after our little brother, Josie. You don't want to be done, after everything that's happened today?"

"I want to be. But do you really think Goodrich is done with us?"

Fox was silent for too long. And that was answer enough.

AFTER ANOTHER RESTLESS NIGHT, I FOUND Mason and Fox at the breakfast table with bowls of cold cereal in front of them. They seemed tired but less rattled than the night before, eating in their usual reckless hurry so they could have seconds and thirds. I grabbed a piece of toast from a plate on the counter. "Where's Aunt Barb?"

"Packing a few things Dad wanted," Fox said. "We're going to the hospital as soon as she's ready."

My heart did a tiny flip inside my chest. "We get to see him? That's great!"

"And no school," Mason added.

I sighed in relief. "Good."

I noticed a huge basket on the table, packed with home-made cinnamon bread, oatmeal chocolate chip cookies, raspberry jam, and several puzzle books.

"She baked," Fox said.

"I see that."

Aunt Barb cooked when under stress. I wondered how

late she'd stayed up—or how long she'd been awake. The kitchen still smelled like brown sugar and cinnamon. My stomach rumbled. "She leave any for us?"

He gestured to a tray of cookies cooling beside the stove. I abandoned my toast and took a cookie instead.

As I ate, I watched Mason on the sly to see how he was dealing with everything. He was no longer shoveling in bites of cereal but chewed slowly staring off into space.

Aunt Barb bustled in, freshly showered and dressed. Her gardenia perfume made my eyes water as she kissed me hello.

The boys jumped up. "Time to go?"

I grabbed my coat and two more cookies before joining them at the door.

"Yes, yes, my goodness. I'm coming. Eager to see your daddy, are you?" She smiled. "I think he's eager to see you, too."

The phone rang.

"Bother," she said as she reached to answer it. "I'll be two minutes, tops."

Aunt Barb hated cell phones. She refused to use one. But she did install an extralong cord on the home phone so she could talk and do pretty much anything else at the same time.

I strained my ears to listen in between bites of cookie.

"Well, no," Aunt Barb was saying. "No, I don't know what you—how did you hear about that?"

She wandered into the next room, out of eavesdropping range. She came back a few minutes later, her face red.

"Honestly, the people in this town get hold of a piece of gossip and they gobble it up for breakfast, lunch, and dinner."

Fox and I avoided looking at each other to keep from laughing out loud. Aunt Barb was probably just sore that whatever news it was hadn't come from her. "Now, let's get these dishes cleared . . . "

The phone rang again.

"Now who . . . ?"

She spent the next hour on the phone while we sat slumped on the couch with our coats on, waiting.

Word had gotten out, about a lot of things.

People wanted to know how Dad was, if the auction was still on for this weekend, if there was anything they could do to help. But mostly they wanted to know if it was true that we'd landed the Goodrich estate.

Aunt Barb worked herself into a righteous fury. After a dozen conversations, she ripped the phone cord right out of the wall. "Have they no shame?" she fumed as she slid her arms into her puffy coat sleeves and gathered up her basket for Dad. "Honestly, you'd think they'd have something better to do."

Fox and I held our tongues as she marched us out the door.

* * *

Taking that first step through the hospital doors brought a rush of sights and sounds I'd tried hard to forget. People in scrubs or white doctor's coats hurried through the halls. The families of sick people walked slower, as if their feet were weighed down with dread. A frail old woman in a flimsy hospital gown shuffled along one wall, pushing her IV pole ahead of her on squeaky wheels.

The boys moved closer to me until we formed an awkward cluster. I counted the tile squares on the floor so I didn't have to see inside people's rooms as we passed them.

But when we got to Dad's room, he looked much better than I'd expected. He was sitting up in bed, his leg casted foot to knee and propped on a mound of pillows.

Uncle Bill looked worse, hat askew, flannel shirt rumpled from sleeping in a chair. He gave us all distracted hugs before Aunt Barb bustled him down to the cafeteria for a break while we crowded around Dad and basked in his tired smile.

"Glad to see your clumsy old dad?" He had black-and-green bruises down one side of his face and peppering his arms.

Mason tried climbing right into the bed a few times. Fox handed him the TV remote to distract him.

"When do they spring you?" Fox asked.

"Tomorrow, probably, or the next day. They just want to make sure I don't disturb all the fancy hardware they put in my leg." He shifted in the bed with a wince.

"Are you thirsty? Can I get you anything?" I poured a cup of water from a plastic pitcher and set it in front of him.

He glanced at the TV channels flying past under Mason's quick thumb. "No good sports in this place. Food's not much to write home about, either. Don't suppose you have a *Sports Illustrated* and a bucket of chicken wings in that basket, do you?"

"Sorry. Aunt Barb brought you plenty of baked goods to tide you over, though," I said as brightly as I could.

"And some puzzle books," Fox added, his voice as full of phony cheer as my own.

"And I made you a card," Mason said, eyes still glued to the TV.

"Well, now, you three are very thoughtful."

We fell silent as we ran out of small talk. I wondered if Dad remembered what he'd seen in the Goodrich house. I wanted to ask, but I wasn't sure how to bring it up. Maybe he hadn't seen anything. Bumping his head could have caused him to say strange things.

He seemed in good spirits, but a few times I watched him when he thought no one was looking. There was something in his eyes, a haunted look that had never been there before.

"So is the business surviving without me?" he asked. "Uncle Bill will grab the truck from Clark this afternoon. He'll need to get some photos posted online, get a preview together for Saturday's auction."

"You're not going to cancel?" I asked.

"Can't. We have other estates lined up. We can't afford to get a week behind. We're thinking of having the newspaper do a write-up about the Goodrich estate, maybe on Wednesday, get the word out without causing too much fuss."

"Dad," Fox said, "word's already out. People were calling the house all morning."

His face fell. "I should have known. I suppose it's just a matter of time before . . ."

"Jim!" Aunt Barb burst into the room. "Look who we ran into in the hall."

Brothers and auction regulars Carl and Joe, looking as out of place as pigs in a pool hall, stood in the doorway, one of them holding a yellow smiley face balloon even though his own expression was as dour as ever.

"Hello there, fellas!" Dad said.

The tiny room, already crowded with Fox, Mason, and me, now felt stifling. We stood squished against the far wall as the small talk began anew. It quickly turned from "So sorry about your unfortunate accident" to "Since we're such good customers, how about you let us have a preview of that Goodrich estate?"

Barb sent them on their way soon enough. "We're going, too. Kids, say your goodbyes now. Your daddy needs his rest if he's to come home to us as quick as he can."

"You'll be seeing more of Mitch until my cast comes off," Dad said when I hugged him. "You liked him, right, guys?" I nodded; Fox shrugged. "Nice young fellow, good to have around. Bill is arranging it all. He found someone else to keep an eye on the Goodrich home. You three help Mitch and Uncle Bill out where they need you, all right?"

Dad hugged Fox next. "You help your aunt and your sister, understand?" Fox nodded. "And keep a lid on those moneymaking schemes," Dad added with a wink. "Josie, you'll keep him in line, won't you?"

"I'll try."

"What about me, Dad?" Mason demanded, making one more attempt to climb up on the bed. Aunt Barb wrapped both arms across his chest to keep him still.

"Your job is to help your aunt set up a space for me in the living room. I won't be going up and down stairs for a while. Okay?"

Mason nodded and threw his arms around Dad's neck. I remembered Mason's terrified screams and my own pounding heart as we'd rushed to him the night before, not knowing what we'd find.

With my family gathered in that cramped room, I felt a pang of love and fear and loss. Momma's death had left a jagged, painful hole in our lives, but it had brought us closer together, too. I vowed that nothing was going to ruin the happiness we had left.

We left the hospital mostly in good spirits, thankful that Dad seemed okay, relieved that nothing strange had happened since the night before.

We kept so busy the rest of the day that I found myself wishing I'd gone to school instead.

Fox and I spent hours uploading photos to the computer and adding them to the Fletcher Auctions website. I was pretty comfortable with computers, so a few years back, Dad had appointed me official website administrator. It was way less glamorous than it sounded.

Uncle Bill wrote item descriptions and a paragraph about the Goodrich family, struggling for the right balance between respectful and "Don't miss this once-in-a-lifetime sale!" Fox helped him spice it up a little—just enough to draw in customers instead of lulling them into a coma.

Working in the storeroom, I kept jumping at the slightest sound. My neck and shoulders grew stiff. I found myself humming Momma's favorite song, "You Are My Sunshine," to fill the silence.

Uncle Bill had discovered the shattered lights. He scratched his head but otherwise didn't question it. Just went and got new bulbs and the extra tall ladder and replaced them.

At one point, I spotted the shadow box and books we'd left behind the night before. I hid them in a closet to keep them from being sold. Just in case.

Late in the afternoon, we were on a snack break—Aunt Barb's homemade scones with honey—when someone knocked at the kitchen door. It was Marcus Crabtree, a regular customer at Fox's auctions who was a year older than me and who walked like a gorilla. Fox didn't open the door but motioned through the window for Marcus to meet us out at the Cave.

Aunt Barb was on the phone again. We mouthed that we were going outside, and she waved us away. We grabbed our coats and jogged out to where Marcus waited, clutching a foot-tall statue of Elvis in one huge fist.

"I want my money back, Fletcher. This thing isn't haunted and you know it. It hasn't moved once since I overpaid you for it two weeks ago." His words reminded me that Fox was due to hold another "haunted" auction soon. Now that we were being haunted for real, it seemed pointless and childish.

Fox took the statue and examined it from head to toe. "Hmmm. Now, we do have a strict no-return policy, but it's bad business to have an unhappy customer. Would you consider trading it for another item?"

"I just want my money."

"You did exactly what I told you, right? Kept it in a darkened room, away from direct sunlight? The owner was a coal miner when he was still alive. Couldn't stand bright light."

"How am I supposed to see if it does anything if it's in a dark room? I carried it around with me in my backpack."

"Ah, now, there's your second problem," Fox said. "The owner was claustrophobic; he didn't like small, confined spaces."

"How can a miner be claustrophobic, moron?"

"Your guess is as good as mine. But what you need is dark, open space for this piece. Under those conditions, the statue is guaranteed to move at least once, if not every night."

Marcus sneered. "It only moves at night? So what—I gotta stay up all night to see if it does anything?"

"How many ghosts come out in the middle of the day?" Fox said.

"Well, none—"

"Okay, then. Take the statue home, give it two more weeks under the conditions I specified, and you're sure to see results."

"Look, Fletcher, I think you're full of it. Now, maybe if you'd let me trade this for something from the Goodrich estate . . ."

There it was.

"My family is auctioning the Goodrich estate, not me." Fox's smooth tone gained a brittle edge.

"What was in that old house of theirs, anyway?" Marcus said. "I heard that old geezer was a hoarder, that the place was crawling with roaches."

I could tell Fox wanted to take on this idiot. On a normal day he would probably have used jokes and flattery to tame the guy's nasty temperament, but today Fox's green eyes were stormy, like he was itching for something to hit, and Marcus was the perfect target. But Marcus was also a foot taller than Fox and twice as wide.

"I'm so sorry, Marcus, but I've just remembered something I have to do. Would you excuse us?" He tried to push past the bigger boy, but Marcus put out a pudgy hand to stop him.

"No. I came here to get my money back, or at the very least get some good dirt on the Goodrich place, and I've just decided I'm not leaving without both."

The mood in the tiny room shifted. It felt closer, darker, like storm clouds closing in. The air grew cold.

I'd never seen Fox in a situation he couldn't talk his way out of. But Marcus wasn't backing down. I was glancing around for something I could use as a weapon if the need arose when:

BANG!

The door blew open with a sound like a gunshot. It closed again with the same violence. Over and over the door flew open and shut, open and shut.

Our breath clouded the air around us. The table in the center of the room began to rattle and tremble.

"What's going on?" Marcus said. He advanced again on Fox, statue raised threateningly. "You think your little tricks will help—"

The window shattered inward. Glass flew everywhere. We threw ourselves flat on the ground, covering our heads. Fox and I tried to take refuge under the table, but it shook so much we couldn't get near it. Something ripped the statue out of Marcus's hand. It flew across the room and crashed into one wall, then the opposite wall.

The head shattered. Now jagged and deadly, it hovered in the air above Marcus, as if someone stood poised to take a swing at him.

Marcus ran. Out the door, through the trees, and out of sight.

We stood and edged toward the door, watchful for any new threats, but the statue fell harmlessly to the floor. The table stilled. The door snicked shut.

Fox and I stared at the statue, then at each other. I reached over and brushed bits of glass from his hair.

"I'm guessing that was Goodrich," I said, my voice not quite steady. "Did he just . . . save us?"

He scratched his head. "Looks like."

"How can this be happening?" I squeezed my eyes shut as I counted to ten in my head. "If that *was* Goodrich, he obviously doesn't need the cameras to get through to us. What does he want?"

Fox sat down at the table, drumming his fingers on the scarred surface. "In the storeroom, he kept saying 'save them.' It was written on that paper from the safe, too. Maybe he's hung up on the fact that he and his wife couldn't stop the landslide. Maybe he still thinks it's 1975. I mean, he died an old man, but in the Polaroids, he looks like he did back then. I wonder . . ." He jumped up and headed for the door.

"Where are you going?"

"I'll be right back. I just want to try something."

"Wait, don't—" I started, but he was already off and running toward the house. "Leave me here alone," I finished, wrinkling my nose at the glass scattered across the floor.

I was scraping the glass into the corner with my shoe when Fox returned with a Polaroid camera hanging around his neck.

"You're kidding," I said. "You're the one who said you wanted to be done with this, remember? Where did you get that?"

"Coat closet. There was a whole box of old cameras in there, just like Dad said. I'm surprised Mason hasn't gotten to them yet."

"What's it for?"

"So far we've only seen Goodrich through items that he owned—his TVs, his cameras. I wanted to see what happened if we used our own camera."

Why not? I thought, slumping down in the nearest chair to watch.

Fox checked for film, and when he didn't find any, he pointed the camera at the wall and pressed the button.

A photo slid out and fell to the floor.

"How is he doing that?" I yelled, nudging the picture with my toe. The same familiar image of Goodrich appeared soon after.

At least his lips weren't moving.

"Guess he's got a thing for cameras," Fox said. "Old ones, anyway."

A burst of laughter escaped me before I knew it was coming.

Fox looked at me like I'd lost my mind. "What?"

"I was just thinking about the look on Marcus's face."

Fox snickered. "Think he'll be back?"

"Nope."

A breath of wind gusted through the broken window, stealing away the lighter mood.

"So . . . what now?" I said. "This has to stop. Goodrich could have killed Marcus with that statue."

"Seems like he could hurt any of us if he really wanted to, but he hasn't."

"Not yet. What about all this glass? We're lucky we didn't get cut. And what about Mason? He was so scared, Fox."

"I know." Fox jammed his hands into his pockets. "If we could just figure out what the guy wants. 'Save them' isn't enough to go on."

I sat up a little taller. "Eva."

"Who?"

"Aunt Barb's hairdresser. She worked right there in the Goodrich house for years. Maybe she knows something."

He fussed with the camera around his neck. "Isn't that the lady who says she saw Mothman?"

I nodded. "Is that a problem?"

"It just sounds so . . . out there."

"People would probably say that about us if we told them what we've seen."

He snorted. "That's true."

"Let's just go talk to her, hear her out. What could it hurt?"

"Okay," Fox said. "I'm in. What time is it?"

I checked my phone. "Almost five."

"Too late to go see her today. How about tomorrow after school?"

"Oh, wait. Dad might come home tomorrow."

"We'll have to find a good excuse to sneak away."

My heart sank. "But I want to see Dad."

"I do, too, Josie. We'll do both. Are you in?"

I thought of Mason's screams and Dad's bruised, tired face. I remembered my resolve at the hospital that I wouldn't let anything else harm my family.

I stood to face him. "I'm in."

AT SCHOOL THE NEXT DAY, SEVERAL KIDS
told me they were sorry about my dad; twice as
many asked about the Goodrich house. One kid even
wanted to know if a ghost had been responsible for Dad's
accident. I told him off, loudly, right there in the hall,
partly because he was an insensitive jerk, and partly because the reason for Dad's fall was a topic Fox and I had
been avoiding.

On the bus ride home, I bounced in my seat, knowing
I would beat the boys by thirty minutes and glad for the
extra time with Dad, if he was home. I willed the bus to
go faster, smiling when I saw Uncle Bill's car parked in
front of the house.

I ran inside and flung my book bag and coat on the
floor. I found Aunt Barb and Uncle Bill perched on the
couch, their faces pinched, hands fidgeting.

My steps faltered. "Where's Dad?"

"Hey, Josie," Aunt Barb said with a forced smile.
"How was your day?"

"Fine. Where's Dad?" I checked the kitchen and the bathroom on the unlikely chance he was waiting to jump out and surprise me.

"Why don't you sit down for a minute, honey?"

My insides froze, squeezed, shattered. "Where's Dad?" I shouted.

Aunt Barb stood quickly, hands splayed in a calming gesture. "It's not what you think, honey, okay? He's all right. He's still at the hospital. They just want to keep him a little longer."

I sank into Dad's leather chair and let the tears fall, torn between relief and fear.

Aunt Barb scooted the ottoman beside me and sat down. "There's an infection, Josie. They're fighting it with strong antibiotics, okay? He just has to stay for a few more days. I didn't mean to scare you. I got it all wrong, didn't I?"

I sniffed and wiped the tears from my cheeks. "Kind of."

"I'm sorry, pudding." She squeezed my shoulders in apology.

"So will he be home for the auction?"

"They're not sure. They hope so. But you know your daddy. He would try to get up out of his wheelchair and run the darn thing all by himself. He doesn't need that kind of stress."

"But he'll be okay? Are we going back today to see him?"

"Uncle Bill and I were there all morning. He's very tired. Maybe tomorrow?"

I tried to smile to hide my disappointment. From his spot on the couch, Uncle Bill gave a slow nod—his own special way of offering reassurance. I knew they both tried so hard, did so much for us, and I loved them for it. But I wouldn't feel settled until we got Dad back.

I drifted into the kitchen and helped myself to a couple of peanut butter cookies. I had plenty of homework, but I couldn't bring myself to start it yet. I remembered that Mitch's car had been parked beside Uncle Bill's, so I went out to the auction building to see what he was up to. I found him hauling the large furniture pieces from the storeroom out to the auction floor, arranging them around the perimeter of the room for shoppers to preview. He parked the dolly when he saw me and mopped his forehead with one sleeve.

"Hey there, Josie. Nice to see you again."

"You too."

"How's your dad?"

"He has to stay at the hospital a few more days."

"Aw, that's a shame."

I nodded. "They've already put you to work, I see."

"Yes, ma'am. It beats sitting out at that house all alone, watching for trespassers."

"Did you ever catch any?"

"Two or three. Sent them on their way pretty quick."

I could imagine. Mitch was built like a bodyguard.

"So how did you end up working for my dad?"

He smiled. "Good story, actually. I'm taking a semester off from the university because—well, because I'm trying to earn some tuition money. The Goodrich lawyer, Mr. Latimer, is a friend of my dad's. He hired me to do some landscaping on the property, get it cleaned up some, but John Goodrich died just a few weeks after I started. I thought that was the end of it, but I happened to be up there working when your dad first came to inventory the estate. He saw my OU sweatshirt, we got to talking about basketball, and the next thing I knew he was offering me a job working security."

"That sounds like Dad."

"It's good money, and I don't have to break my back hauling brush and chopping up dead trees anymore."

"Wow. Now you're hauling furniture instead of trees. Not so sure that's a step up."

He laughed. "At least I get to talk to you and your family. You're all so nice. Grab that door for me, would you?"

I did, then followed him out to the auction floor. As he walked on ahead I noticed he was wearing two different socks—one yellow, one green.

"Hey, Mitch. What's with the socks?"

"These," he said, holding up one ankle, "are my lucky socks. My old high school basketball team is playing in a tournament tonight. If they win, they'll play for the state championship here in Athens next week."

"Do the socks work?"

"Sometimes. But if the team loses and I wasn't wearing my socks, I would feel like it was kind of my fault, you know? I have to do my part."

"Sure."

I bit my lip, wondering if I could be doing more to fix the weirdness plaguing our family the past several days. Suddenly I felt the urge to ask him what I couldn't bring myself to ask Dad. "Mitch? Did you ever see anything strange out at the Goodrich place?"

He shifted a rolltop desk into position and headed back to the storeroom for another piece. "Strange . . . you mean ghosts? Have the kids at school been bothering you about that? Because the answer is no. I never saw any ghosts up there."

I plowed ahead with my next question before I could change my mind. "What about Mothman?"

He stopped midstep and turned back to stare at me.

"Now there's an odd question. I thought that guy was connected with Point Pleasant."

"Yeah. Yeah, I guess so."

A smile tugged at the corners of his mouth. "Sorry, Josie. Not a single ghost, Mothman, zombie, or unicorn. Just the occasional deer or raccoon."

I felt my face grow hot. I wanted to sink into the floor.

He must have noticed, because he put a hand on my shoulder and said, "I'm sorry. I didn't mean to give you a hard time. I just don't believe in that stuff. I gotta get back to work now, okay?"

Between Mitch's teasing and my disappointment at not seeing Dad, my mood was in freefall. I just wanted to be alone.

I stomped to my room and slammed the door, not bothering to say hello to Fox and Mason or wait around for their reaction to the news about Dad. I took out the lockbox. I found the moth stickpin and set it on my dressing table. Then I sat down and met my own eyes in the mirror, daring myself to put on the pin to see if anything would happen.

I let my fingers hover over the pin, then scooped it up and wrapped both hands around it. The cold metal bit into my skin like a shard of ice. I held it for as long as I could stand it, the cold biting deeper, sharper, watching my features twist in the mirror as my hands took the abuse.

At last, with a quick yelp of pain, I dropped the pin. It bounced and rattled across the table. I watched, transfixed, as it traveled the entire surface before falling to the carpet with a muted thump. I thought about leaving it there; my hand still ached from holding it. But I didn't want anyone else to find it. Sighing, I crawled under the dressing table to retrieve it, a sleeve stretched over my palm to blunt the chill.

"Josie?"

I jumped. My head hit the underside of the table.

"Ouch!"

"Josie?" Fox's voice drifted through the door. "You in there?"

I slipped the pin into my pocket just as he peeked in. "Josie, hey, do you—what are you doing down there?"

"Nothing. I dropped something." I crawled out, rubbing the tender spot on the back of my head. "What's up?"

"You heard about Dad, I guess."

"Yeah."

He hesitated. "You still want to go see that hairdresser today? We could make it there and back on our bikes before dinner."

"Okay. Maybe she'll be more helpful than Mitch was."

"Mitch? What do you mean?"

I sank down on the edge of my bed. "Oh, nothing. I asked him about Mothman, and he practically laughed in my face."

"Why did you do that, Josie? Of course he laughed."

"It doesn't matter. He's not going to tell anyone. He thinks I'm just a stupid kid."

Fox sat down beside me. "No, he doesn't. Some people just can't handle talking about supernatural stuff."

"I'm pretty sure Aunt Barb's hairdresser isn't one of those people. Let's go."

* * *

Mason was so disappointed about Dad not coming home that Aunt Barb had to bribe him with cookies and a few "new" broken electronics to keep him happy.

Fox assured Aunt Barb with a straight face that we were going to the library to catch up on homework. She even packed us a snack.

It was a three-mile ride, but we found the beauty salon easily enough. It was just down the street from the Supercuts where Dad always took us.

As we locked up our bikes, Fox said, "If she's here, she'll be working. She can't just take time off to answer

a bunch of questions. You have to get her to cut your hair. She'll talk the whole time."

I clutched my twin braids. "I don't know, Fox." When Momma was sick and lost her hair, I cut mine short so she wouldn't feel so bad. She'd caught me with scissors in hand and a pile of my hair in the bathroom sink. We cried, and then we laughed, and for a little while it seemed like everything might be okay. When she died, it took me a year to start letting it grow out again. It took another two years to get it this long, and I was too ashamed to admit that I liked the way it looked, a rich wheat color, thick and shiny. I liked how I could toss it casually over my shoulder, flash a smile, and pretend for a moment that I was as confident as Fox.

"C'mon, Josie. You don't have to get it chopped off; just get a trim." He gave me his hurt puppy look. "Pleee-ase? It's for the greater good."

I peeked through the window at the prices posted on the wall. "It will take the last of our money. A haircut here is twenty-two dollars plus tip."

"Aunt Barb will pay us back. Just tell her you've been needing one but it got overlooked, so to take some of the burden off her you went on ahead and took care of it. One less thing for her to worry about."

"You're evil."

"Thank you," he said.

"Why don't you do it? You'd do a better job asking questions anyway."

"I just got a haircut two weeks ago. It's perfect just like it is."

"You look like a politician."

He checked his reflection in the storefront glass, his face hopeful. "Really?"

"Oh, forget it. I'll do it."

We marched inside.

A woman looked up from behind the register and smiled broadly. She must have been my grandma's age, but she was the prettiest, most stylish grandma I'd ever seen. She had high cheekbones and perfectly arched eyebrows. Her black hair was piled high on her head, her lips painted a glossy pink. "*Kumusta ka*, my beautiful children! How is your poor father?" She tsked. "Such a terrible accident, and in such a place, too."

We stopped short. "You know us?" I said.

"Of course! Your auntie shows me your photographs every time she comes in. I am Eva." She approached with arms wide and engulfed us both in a huge hug. "Thank the good Lord your father is on the mend. What brings you to my shop today, all on your own? Where is your auntie?"

"She's at home with our little brother. I've been wanting a trim, so . . ."

"Of course! The girl is becoming more a woman every day! Let Eva have a look."

Fox smirked as he chose a magazine and settled into one of the orange plastic chairs by the front window.

"It's good that you caught me. It's been so slow today I was going to close early. I let the other girls go home already." She sat me down and let out my braids. She finger-combed my tousled hair. "Mm, it is a little dry. This will not help to catch a handsome young man someday."

I felt a blush creep up my ears. Up front I saw Fox hide a mocking grin behind his *National Geographic*.

"We will deep condition, clean up these split ends, perhaps add some layers to frame that pretty face of yours." She fussed and chatted as she washed my hair and worked about a gallon of conditioner through it. Once I was rinsed and in the chair, she asked again about our dad, and I knew it was the best opening I could hope for.

"He has to stay at the hospital for a few more days. You know, we were with him when it happened, Fox and me."

She gasped. "I didn't know. My poor dears. Some things were not meant for children's eyes. Why would your father take you to such a place?" As she combed the tangles from my wet hair, her movements grew rougher, more vigorous. I clenched my teeth to keep from yelping in pain.

"We were helping get ready for the auction this weekend. It was a pretty house, not scary like we pictured."

"Yes. Such a beautiful house. Mmm. But beauty is not everything."

"Eva?"

"Yes, child?"

"Is it true that you worked at the Goodrich place?"

The comb paused. "Your aunt has been talking too much again, I suppose."

"Um . . ." I suddenly wondered if it was such a good idea to get her upset when she would soon have a pair of scissors in her hand.

She grunted. "Yes. I worked there. Before the tragedy *and* after." She made the sign of the cross with her free hand. "Mr. Goodrich was forever changed. He was a cheerful, kind man. But losing his wife, his town—it would change anyone. He withdrew, spoke rarely. But after dark he would talk to Nora, late into the night."

"Talk to . . . his dead wife?"

She traded the comb for scissors and started snipping, her expert fingers in constant motion. "Yes. It brought him peace, although his talks would sometimes grow angry, accusing."

I lost all interest in watching pieces of my hair fall to the floor. "Did . . . did she talk back?"

She laughed. "No, child."

"Because she wasn't really there. Right?"

She didn't answer.

"Eva?"

At last she spoke, her voice low and intense. "Talk of spirits is best left alone, Josephina. I have forgotten myself. Just be thankful your father will recover."

Apparently that was all she wanted to say.

I had to up the stakes, make the conversation impossible for her to resist. But how much to tell her? Like with Aunt Barb, a secret would not stay secret long with Eva, I was sure.

I plunged ahead. "Could a spirit make my dad fall down the stairs?"

She slammed the scissors down on the counter and crossed herself once more. "Such questions!"

"I have to know. Did other bad things happen in the house? Is that why you quit?"

"I did not quit, child. I was let go—for this very reason, no less!" She picked up the scissors again and pointed them at me.

"For . . . ?"

"Not knowing how to keep private affairs *private*."

"Oh."

She worked in silence for the next few minutes. I gave up hope of finding out anything more and kept my gaze on my lap, but once our eyes met in the mirror, she seemed to sigh and come to a decision.

She leaned in close to my ear. "Plenty of bad things happened in that house. Perhaps you deserve to know the truth. Perhaps then you will know enough to stay far away from it."

I nodded, quickly rearranging my expression from eager to solemn, trying not to draw attention to the fact that Fox had moved closer so he wouldn't miss a word.

"Mrs. Goodrich was once a mild person, very quiet and content. Several years before the landslide, she became obsessed with disasters. She kept newspaper clippings about them. She was often fearful and unhappy. Then, about a year before the landslide, she got much worse. People thought her mind was beginning to unravel."

Eva paused to plug in the hair dryer. We had little time left to talk. I spoke up to speed things along. "Why would they think that, Eva?"

"She would fly into a rage over the smallest things, or cry for hours on end. She would stir up trouble in town, trying to warn people that they were in danger. But they would not listen. She grew more and more upset, raving about the bridge disaster in Point Pleasant. John tried to help but did not know how."

I thought about the scrapbook Fox had found, every page filled with disaster stories. "Point Pleasant, huh? Isn't that where all those Mothman sightings were reported?"

The scissors clattered to the floor. It took a minute or two for her to retrieve them, plunk them into a glass jar of sterilizer, and choose a new pair. "You are a smart young woman, Josephina. Smart enough to know better than to open up this can of worms, as they say."

I kept pushing. "So you've heard of Mothman, then?"

"Of course."

"Some people say you've seen him."

She grew still. Her gaze flickered to the shop window. She stared at a traffic signal, its single red eye flashing. "I never saw him in the house," she whispered. "But sometimes at the windows. Only glimpses here and there, but yes."

"What about in the town?"

"People spoke of him in the months before the landslide. A few saw him outright; most dismissed it as fantasy."

Fox and I stared at each other.

"Do you know where Mothman came from? Why he was there?"

"It started with a piece of jewelry. Nora had a half sister in Point Pleasant who died in the bridge accident. Months later, she received a package from the sister's estate with jewelry and other personal effects."

"How do you know it was the jewelry?"

"There was one piece in particular with a most unusual design: a gold pin with a moth preserved under glass." In the mirror I watched the color drain from my face. My grip tightened on the arms of the chair.

Eva didn't notice. "Mrs. Goodrich believed that pin was the origin of Mothman, dating back a hundred years or more. Stories tell of a man who dealt in dark magic to preserve his own life, and to punish a lost love." The scissors stilled. She leaned in close. "And it is said," she whispered, "that the pin brings a curse upon the person who possesses it."

8

SUDDENLY I COULDN'T BREATHE, AS IF A hand had closed around my throat and started to squeeze.

"Goodness, are you all right?"

I couldn't speak, so I nodded instead, but she didn't believe me.

Eva's voice became steel. "Fox! Fox Fletcher!"

He yelped and dropped his magazine.

"You come here this instant! I know you are listening."

Fox stood and inched closer, but stayed several paces out of arm's reach.

"Why so many questions? You would allow your younger sister to pursue evil such as this?"

I found enough breath to clear up an important point. "I'm—actually, I'm older—"

"Something is wrong with her. Do you see her face?"

His eyebrows drew together as he studied me. "Yeah, I do. Josie?"

I shook my head at him, signaling him to ease off, but Eva's tirade continued. "What are you up to? The both of you?" Fox actually shrank back as she started up a lecture in her native language. I couldn't be sure, but a lot of it sounded like curse words.

"Have you seen the pin?" she demanded.

"N-no," I lied. "But if someone did find it, couldn't they just throw it away?"

"It would make no difference. Wherever the pin turns up, calamity follows. The owner of the pin must stop it, or the curse lives on, and people will die."

Now I really couldn't breathe. Sharp claws of panic seized my chest. So I did the logical thing.

I ran for the bathroom and locked myself in.

* * *

"Josie. Come on out of there. Josie?" Fox's fists pounded on the door.

My teeth chattered. My wet, half-finished hair hung in my eyes. A curse? What kind of curse? What did she mean by "calamity follows"? Was my family in danger? The whole town? I paced a two-foot path, back and forth, trying not to touch anything in the tiny room.

I remembered a similar panic when Momma died. I'd crawled under my bed and sobbed until I couldn't breathe, until Dad came and held me and smoothed my hair.

"Josie!" *Pound, pound, pound.* I pulled the pin from my pocket, clutching it tight enough to leave marks on my skin, to feel the bite of the icy-cold metal. I unfolded my fingers to stare at the ugly thing. Eva had said the curse couldn't be broken by throwing the pin away. What if I flushed it? Was that the same thing? Or I could break it. Surely others had tried that, right? Still, it was worth a shot.

I dropped the pin and ground my heel into it. I pictured glass splintering and shredding the dried-up moth beneath it. I listened for the satisfying crunching sound it would make against the tile floor. It never came.

"Josie? You better be decent in there because we're coming in." A key rattled in the lock. The door flung inward to reveal Eva and Fox standing on the threshold looking winded and worried.

I shoved the wet hair out of my face and tried to take deep, even breaths. "I'm okay," I told them. "I'm okay. You were right, Eva. I take those scary stories way too seriously. Hey, Eva, could I talk to my brother real quick? I just need a minute. We'll be right out. I promise."

She stared me down, eyes searching my face for the truth. A truth I couldn't bear to confess to anyone but Fox. She nodded and left us alone. As soon as the door swung shut, I lifted my foot and stepped back. The pin lay gleaming on the tile, whole and undamaged.

"Is that—?" Fox crouched down for a closer look.

"Oh, no. Josie—oh, man. Where did you get this? Why didn't you tell me?"

"I found it after Dad fell. It must have been in the safe with all those papers." I hung my head. "I had a feeling something wasn't right about it."

He reached to pick it up. "Don't!" I shouted, diving for the pin myself. I stood and backed away, cradling the pin in my hands. "What if it curses you, too?"

He straightened but kept his distance, his face wary. "Is that what Eva said?"

"She said whoever possesses it."

"Well, that's specific. You believe her, then? You really think it's cursed?"

I looked down at my clasped hands, suddenly realizing where the pin had been. I made a face and hurried to the sink, running the pin and my hands under a stream of hot water. "Two minutes ago I tried to squash this into bits with my shoe, and there's not a scratch on it," I said. "Yeah. I'd say it's cursed." I shook the pin dry and put it back in my pocket, out of sight.

Fox ran both hands through his hair. "So Mrs. Goodrich owned the pin. She and her husband tried to stop a major disaster in Clark, and failed. She got the pin from her sister, who died in a major disaster in Point Pleasant."

"And Point Pleasant is famous for its Mothman

sightings," I finished. "According to Eva, Mothman was seen in Clark, too, and this curse of his is linked to the terrible things that happened. Sound about right?"

"So is he causing the disasters? Trying to stop them?" Fox wondered. "Or something else?"

"I don't know," I said, shivering. My hair lay heavy and cold around my shoulders. The pin sat like a stone in my pocket. I folded my arms across my stomach. "What do I do?"

"*We* figure this out together," he said. "And we stay here until we get the whole story from Eva."

I swallowed and nodded. "Thanks, Fox." I peeked out the door. Eva stood, hands on hips, jaw set. "Seems like maybe she's done talking, though."

We left the bathroom. I sat back down in the beautician's chair like nothing had happened. Fox claimed the chair next to me. We all stared at each other in awkward silence. Finally, Fox said, "Please, Eva, you have to tell us more."

"I will do no such thing. I have said far too much already."

Eva stayed stubbornly silent as she finished up the haircut and dried my hair. Through the front window I watched a bank of black clouds swallow up the sky outside.

Lightening flashed. Seconds later, a rumble of thunder followed, and then the skies opened.

I groaned. A nice, three-mile bike ride in the rain.

Eva patted my shoulder. "Don't worry. I will take you home."

I nearly cried with relief.

* * *

We somehow squeezed our bikes into the trunk of Eva's tiny car. The ride home was quiet, thick tension weaving around us like fog. Raindrops pelted the wind-shield and pounded the car roof, running down the windows in little rivers. It looked as though the car was weeping.

Eva spoke only when we arrived, turning to face us over the driver's seat.

"You have more questions," she said. "I see them in your faces."

"Just one," Fox said. "Did John and Nora live in Clark when they inherited the pin?"

"Yes," she said. "Somehow they knew there would be a disaster, years before it happened. They tried every-thing they could think of to stop it." Her eyes filled with tears. "Some things they told me; many they did not. I stayed with Mr. Goodrich after the town was lost, after his wife passed. Such a terrible time. He said someday another disaster would come. For years I stayed, until he sent me away."

When she finished, we reached for the door handles,

unsure of what else to say. But then I thought of one final thing I had to know. "Mr. Goodrich—he was a good man, wasn't he?"

"Yes. He always tried to do what was right, sometimes at great personal cost."

I mulled this over, remembering his worried face and desperate eyes.

"Please, please be careful, my children," she said in parting. "Stay far away from this."

We thanked her, climbed out of the car to retrieve our bikes, and made a run for the garage to escape the downpour.

By unspoken agreement we stashed our bikes and went straight to the Cave to figure out our next move.

We sat across from each other, the pin on the table between us. We stared at it. I drummed my fingers on the scarred tabletop, tapped my foot, cleaned my nails, twisted a strand of hair around my finger. Fox sat perfectly still. His patience set my teeth on edge.

"I don't know what we're waiting for," I complained. "It's not like the pin is going to start talking to us or anything."

Fox had already done a web search on his phone for *cursed moth pin* and found exactly nothing.

"I'm just gonna put it on," I said suddenly, at the same time that Fox said: "Maybe you should put it on."

A nervous laugh bubbled out of me. "How else are we gonna find out anything, right? Maybe nothing will happen. Maybe it's all just a story."

I reached for the pin.

"Josie, wait." Fox grabbed my wrist. "What if the curse doesn't kick in unless you put it on? We could still get rid of it."

I'd thought of that, too. Maybe it wasn't too late to drop it in the river, or down the garbage disposal. But I knew it was wishful thinking. Somehow I could feel that the pin had already claimed me. "The truth is we don't know how any of this really works."

"I guess. It's just . . . I could . . . that is, maybe if I . . . ?" I hadn't seen him so tongue-tied since he was eight years old and got caught polishing off an entire pumpkin pie the night before Thanksgiving. "What if I tried it first? Could we share the curse?"

I was so grateful for his offer I almost took him up on it. I wanted to. But just knowing he'd tried made me feel braver. I knew it was time to put on my big-sister shoes. "It's okay, Fox. I'm not sure it *can* be shared. It's really great of you to offer, but I got this."

I closed trembling fingers around the pin, withdrew my arm, and then, before I could change my mind, jabbed it through the collar of my sweatshirt.

"Well?"

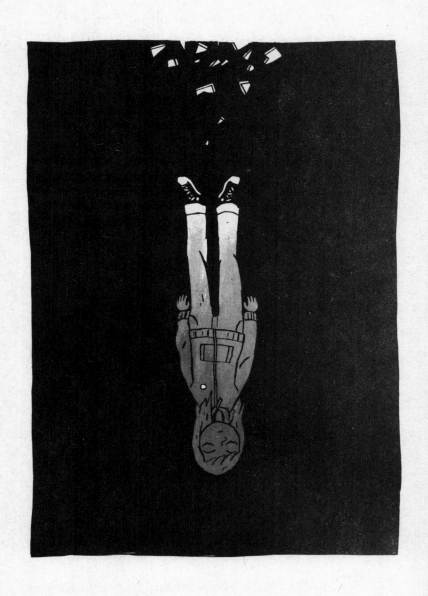

I didn't realize I'd closed my eyes until Fox spoke. Slowly, I opened them and relaxed my tightly clenched fists. I looked left, then right, finally allowing my gaze to settle on Fox's tense face. I felt the corners of my mouth lift, watched his expression mirror my own.

"Nothing's different. I can't see any—"

Red light flared, filling my vision. I flinched, tried to cover my eyes. The air shimmered; light vanished. I saw only watery blackness, as if I'd been plunged into a dark, icy river. It swallowed the room and me along with it. I felt myself falling, falling, Fox's voice calling my name as if from a great distance—

* * *

I was a world away, standing in a grassy field. Two young men were sprawled, lazing in the sunshine, dressed in old-fashioned clothes. One lay on his stomach in the dirt, watching a bug creep along the rocky ground. The other, tall and fair-haired, watched a young woman as she sat on a stone bench nearby, reading a book.

"Edgar, you're missing the best part of the afternoon!" the taller man called.

"I like the view just fine from here, William." Edgar scowled, his dark brows knitting, creasing his angular face.

"You and your bugs," William said, and went back to

watching the woman, his chin in his hands. "Ah, Elsie. There must be some way to capture your attention."

The scene dimmed, rushing past in blurred streaks of light and color and motion.

* * *

Edgar reappeared, a few years older. His wavy hair was slicked back. He stood on a porch, clutching a drooping bunch of wildflowers.

A matronly woman answered the door. "I'm sorry, Edgar. Elsie is out with William this afternoon. Would you like to leave those for her?" she said, reaching for the flowers.

But Edgar snatched them from her reach and crumpled them in his hand. He stormed away, muttering to himself.

* * *

Edgar sat in a dim basement, hunched over a long worktable. He was surrounded by dead bugs of every shape and size, carefully pinned under glass and mounted in dark frames like gruesome trophies. He held delicate tools in his hands as he carefully fashioned a tiny piece of gold jewelry. Edgar kept a running conversation with himself as he worked. "She'll love it. There isn't another like it anywhere. She won't want anything to do with that simpleton William when she sees this." He held it up to the flickering light of an oil lamp. It was a stick-pin. In its center was a moth, preserved under a perfect circle of glass.

* * *

Edgar stood at Elsie's door once more, a hopeful smile softening his face. He wore a dark suit, his slim shoulders thrown back. Elsie graced the open doorway, holding the pin in her outstretched hand. Her full lips shifted from a grimace to a forced smile.

"Edgar Tripp, what a nice . . . gesture. But I'm afraid I can't accept it. My heart belongs to William. It's not your fault, dear. Girls just don't fall for boys like you, with your bugs and your childish ways. I do wish you well. Perhaps we will invite you to the wedding." She moved to hand the pin back but dropped it at the last moment, her smile twisting, eyes unkind. "Oh, dear. Clumsy me." She shut the door in his face.

Edgar bent to retrieve the pin. He cradled it in his palm, then clenched his fingers around it, blinking back tears.

* * *

Once again at his worktable, hair in disarray, Edgar hunched over a paper filled with scrawled handwriting and strange symbols. His lips moved in a whispered chant as he read aloud from the page, the words coming faster, turning to smoke that twisted and writhed from his mouth like a serpent, winding to encircle the pin and lift it into the air, where it began to glow with a white-hot fire.

* * *

Edgar stood in the grassy field, pointing a gun at Elsie and William. William stepped in front of Elsie, his face a mask of fear and disbelief. Edgar's own face was smooth and peaceful.

"I'll give you a choice this one last time, Elsie. I'm only going to kill one of you. Save the life of your beloved William, or save your own. It doesn't matter to me, but I believe you truly love no one but yourself. Prove me wrong."

"Edgar! We were friends. Please don't do this. Please!"

"Do be quiet, William. You were only my friend when you had nothing else to keep you amused for the day."

Elsie looked from one man to the other, her face streaked with tears.

"Quickly, now, Elsie. I'm getting bored."

"I—I choose . . . " She met William's eyes, then looked away. "I choose him. Kill him."

William's eyes filled. "Elsie . . ."

She would not look at William, so he turned to face Edgar, unflinching. "Yes. It should be me. Please, allow her to live, Edgar. Fear compels her. There is unselfishness in her heart. I know there is."

"We will see," Edgar said, and pulled the trigger.

* * *

I gasped, throat raw, lungs heaving. I found myself curled in a ball on the dirty floor of the Cave, Fox kneeling next to me, his face stark, shaking my arm and begging, "Please, Josie, wake up, please, *please*."

I sat up, trembling, my skin icy. I scooted back into the corner and hid my face in my hands.

Fox swiped a sleeve across his eyes and blinked at me. "Josie? Are you in there?"

I nodded, not trusting my voice.

"You want me to get Aunt Barb?" He looked like a little boy, face ghost-pale and tear-streaked. Like the day we put Momma in the ground.

He hadn't cried since, not about anything, not even the day he broke three toes when he dropped a cast iron doorstop on them. Nothing had cracked that perfect facade.

Until now.

I sniffed. "No." I sat up a little straighter and wiped my face with both hands. "I'm okay, Fox. I'm okay."

"Where did you go, Josie? You were out of it for, like, five minutes. I finally took the pin off you, hoping it would wake you up." He pointed to a corner of the Cave where the pin lay gleaming in the dust.

I tried to stop shaking, to make my voice less wobbly, as I explained about Edgar and Elsie, trying not to leave out a single detail. Then we sat side by side against the wall, the heavy silence broken only by the patter of rain on the roof.

"So this Edgar . . . you think he's Mothman?" Fox said.

"Yes. Probably. I saw him making the pin. He must have given it to Elsie after he killed William. I'm guessing that's how the curse started. I think there was more I was supposed to see, but it got cut short." We looked over at the pin.

He scowled and crossed his arms. "You're not putting it on again."

"Fox, there's still so much we don't know. That might be the only way to get the answers."

"No. I won't let you. You looked dead, Josie. You understand? Just forget it. We'll think of something else."

I let my head thump against the wall, too exhausted to argue. I missed Dad. I missed Momma. I wished I'd never heard of Mothman or John Goodrich or their stupid, ugly pin. But none of this was going to go away on its own. Gathering up my resolve, I lunged across the floor on hands and knees, closed my hand around the pin, and shoved it through a thick fold of my hoodie.

"Josie!" Fox shouted, standing over me, green eyes flashing, angrier than I'd ever seen him.

I glared back, defiant. We waited, the seconds ticking by, but nothing happened. We gave it another minute just to be sure. Finally, he sighed and held out a hand to help me up. I reached to take it—

—and saw the ghost of John Goodrich standing behind Fox's shoulder.

9

"AAAAAAAAAAAAAAAAAAH!" I COULDN'T MANAGE anything more intelligent. It was all just too much.

Fox ducked, looking right and left trying to glimpse the threat. "What? What is it?"

"It's *him*," I hissed. I fought the urge to hide under the table.

"Mothman?" He stared all around. "I don't see him."

"Goodrich. He's *right there*!" I pointed. The figure didn't move or speak. Mostly it just looked at me, forlorn, edges muted and smudged as he'd been in the Polaroids, still all in black and white. He wore the same dreadful suit and glasses, too-long hair parted and combed neatly to either side, huge sideburns hugging half his face.

"Why can you see him and I can't?" Fox's gaze fell on the moth pin. Before I could stop him, he grabbed the pin and clipped it to his own shirt. His eyes darted here and there but didn't settle on any one spot. "I still can't see him. Can you?"

"Not anymore," I snapped. I stood and snatched the pin back. Maybe it only worked for the person who was cursed. I took a deep breath. I'd never know unless I tried.

Sure enough, as soon as I put it on, Goodrich reappeared. He was two feet in front of me, lips moving, though no sound came out.

The tiny hairs on the back of my neck stood straight up. "He's trying to say something."

Fox fixed his gaze on me. "What is it?"

"I don't know! I've never played charades with a dead person before!"

Fox leaned in close and whispered, "I think he's here to help, Josie."

I thought about what Eva had said about John Goodrich when he was alive, that he was a good man. Plus his ghost wasn't doing anything scary or destructive at the moment. He was just standing there.

Maybe it was time to take a leap of faith.

"Just try, okay?" Fox said.

I nodded. "Mr. Goodrich?" I squeaked. My voice failed. I swallowed and tried again. "I—I can't understand you."

The man's lips moved even faster. His hands joined in, stretched toward me in a desperate plea. He took a step forward. I took a step back and ran into the door, the knob digging into the small of my back.

"What kind of a curse is this, anyway?" I ranted. "How am I supposed to fix anything if I can't even hear him?"

Fox gave me a push away from the door. "Take it easy, Josie. We don't want to scare the nice ghost away with all the shouting. Take your time. Try yes-or-no questions. Then he can just nod or shake his head."

"Okay." I cleared my scratchy throat. "Mr. Goodrich, in the storeroom you kept saying 'Save them.' Is something bad going to happen? Is there going to be a disaster?"

He gave a vigorous nod.

"How soon?"

He pointed to his wrist, like someone tapping their watch when they wanted you to hurry.

"Today?"

John shook his head.

"Tomorrow?"

Another head shake.

I clenched my fists and turned to Fox. "John and Nora had years, and they still didn't stop the landslide. How are we supposed to—" I broke off, the answer coming to me in a flash of clarity. "The paper from the safe. Remember? It said 'Save them' and had a group of numbers. Maybe it *is* a date. Do you remember what the numbers were?

Fox closed his eyes. "Zero three two three two . . . zero one five."

It took me a few seconds to work it out. "March twenty-third? But that's this Monday!"

"Less than a week away," Fox said.

"Is it Monday, John?" I asked. "Are we supposed to stop a disaster this coming Monday?"

Goodrich nodded.

"Where? What are we supposed to stop?"

His silent monologue started up again, much faster than I could ever hope to translate.

I sighed and slumped down at the table. "This is hopeless."

Fox glanced around for a solution. "Maybe he could write down his answers or something."

"Great. I'll just get him some ghostly paper and an invisible pen and he can get right on that."

Fox rummaged in the cardboard box where we kept odds and ends and came up with a pen and a dog-eared notebook. "Remember the storeroom? He was controlling solid objects, making them float. Maybe he can do it with smaller objects, too, like Marcus's statue. It can't hurt to try." He placed the pen and paper on the table and backed away, gaze shifting around the room. "Mr. Goodrich, where is the disaster supposed to happen?"

John stepped to the table. Instead of reaching for the pen, he lowered his head and closed his eyes, as if concentrating. The pen skidded and jumped a few times, and after several tries John was able to "lift" the pen to the paper, seemingly by thought alone.

We waited, but try after try, he produced only splotchy scribbles on the blank page. John looked as frustrated as we felt. His lips were moving faster than ever.

"What about something bigger, less precise?" I seized the box and started digging. I held up a piece of blue sidewalk chalk like a trophy. "The wall!" I blurted. "Use this on the wall. Would that work?"

John stepped forward again. His eyes fell closed. The chalk lifted straight up out of my hand and into the air and flew toward the wall, where it collided so hard it crumbled into powder.

"Okay, it's okay, we have more," I babbled. Before I could go digging for more chalk another piece floated up and out of the box, this time ending in a gentle kiss to the wall. Fox and I stood wide-eyed as halting strokes of the chalk formed shaky letters across the planks of the Cave.

SAVE THEM. SAVE THEM.

"Yes, we know," I said. "*Where?*"

FIELD HOUSE.

"Field House," Fox echoed. "There's, uh—the field house at Turner High School for track and football practice."

John shook his head and held his arms out to his sides, as far apart as they would go.

"Bigger?" I said. He nodded. "There's the one on the OU campus." The new building was a joint project

between the city and the university. It hosted community events and some sporting events, too. It wasn't as
big as the Convocation Center, where the Bobcats played
basketball, but it could still hold thousands of people.

"So which one is it?" Fox said.

But I knew by the hollow pit in my stomach it was the one on campus, even before Goodrich pointed at me.

"The one at OU," I told Fox. He drew in a breath, his eyes wide.

"John," I said, "were *you* supposed to stop this disaster?"

He nodded.

"But you died before it happened. So . . . you're still cursed?"

He hesitated, then nodded again.

"He says yes," I told Fox.

"Is there any way to break the curse for good?" I said.

He ignored me. The chalk started up again. The same phrases appeared, messier this time.

SAVE THEM
FIELD HOUSE
SAVE THEM
MARCH 23

John's face twisted as if in pain. His image flickered. The chalk fell and shattered.

"What's going on?" Fox said.

"He's losing control for some reason." John's lips were moving double time. I had no hope of following along.

Suddenly he flinched and disappeared. The room began to glow red.

"Josie, what's happening?" Fox demanded.

"He's gone!"

A piece of red chalk rose and began writing, picking up speed, moving across the wall so fast it was a blur of motion and color. More pieces, all of them red, rose from the box to join the first, creating a tangle of scrawled messages filling every free surface. The writing was harsh and ugly, like ragged graffiti.

At last the chalk, worn down to stubs, was flung to the floor. We turned a slow circle, reading the same few phrases again and again:

THEY WILL ALL DIE
You CANNoT STop IT
You WILL DIE WITH THEM

And the most chilling of all, the one that made my vision swim and turned my knees to jelly:

JoSIE FLETCHER,
You ARE MINE MINE MINE

* * *

We stumbled back to the house, soggy and shaken.

Mason met us at the door, bouncing on his toes, tripping over his words, eyes alight. The shock of normal hit me hard after such an upsetting afternoon. "Fox! Josie! Want to see what I'm making?"

He clutched the clock radio Fox had scrounged for him from the storeroom. A tangle of wires trailed out the back. An old flip phone was attached to the top with duct tape.

"That's great, kiddo," I said, trying to muster a smile.

"It's not done yet. Don't you want to know what it does?"

Fox ruffled his hair. "Maybe later, okay?"

Aunt Barb poked her head out of the kitchen, cheeks flushed, her red hair sticking up every which way. "Just in time for dinner. Fox, plates and silverware, please. Josie, you've got drinks. Wash up first. Have you done something different with your hair? How was the library? Homework all done? Your brother's been quite the handful. I'd keep a close eye on your cell phones if I were you."

I felt a twinge of guilt for lying about what we'd been up to, but I also felt glad that Aunt Barb didn't know what we'd gotten ourselves into. She had enough to worry about. And so did we.

* * *

It was the longest dinner in history. I choked down food I didn't feel like eating, pretended to be interested in conversations that didn't matter. I didn't dare look at Fox for fear of collapsing in a fit of tears.

After clearing the table, I ran out to the storeroom and grabbed the books and shadow box I'd stashed. Then, while Aunt Barb settled on the couch with her knitting and Uncle Bill watched *Law & Order* reruns, Fox and I tried to lock ourselves in Dad's study, hoping to do some research on the curse. Mason had other ideas, though. Using his outside voice he demanded to know if we'd seen any more floating objects and if the ghost in our house planned to stick around for a while.

We hurried him into the study and shut the door.

"Shh, Mason, that's a secret, remember?" Fox said.

"I know," Mason said. I searched his face for signs of how he was coping with everything. After the chaos in his room Sunday night, on top of Dad getting hurt, I wondered if he was having nightmares. I'd been too distracted to even ask.

He didn't look scared, though. Just curious. My heart swelled with pride for the little goofball.

We told him the basics: Yes, there was a ghost, but it wanted our help and wouldn't hurt us and didn't plan on staying long.

"What kind of help?" Mason said, his expression eager.

"Um," I said, looking to Fox. "He can't find his way to heaven. If we help him save some people, we think he can finally move on."

"Maybe he can say hello to Momma when he gets there."

Tears burned my eyes. I kissed the side of Mason's head. "Maybe so."

We talked about Momma being in heaven all the time. None of us could bear to think that she wasn't *anywhere* anymore. Now that I knew ghosts were real, that there was an *after*, I felt hopeful I would see her again someday.

It was the one bright spot in this whole jumbled-up mess.

Mason settled himself on the rug to work on his "invention."

Fox and I started with the journals. Our eyes met in surprise when the very first one fell open to an ink drawing of a man with leathery wings and beady red eyes. With an unsteady hand, I skimmed page after page of sketches: some of a human figure in flight, wings outstretched, others of a tall, too-thin creature, all shadows and angles, a fusion of moth and man. Some were bare-chested; others wore tattered robes. Some of the wings looked brittle, others thick and tough. Many sketches had dimensions of height and wingspan labeled in number of feet. I flipped to find a signature inside the front cover of the journal: *J. Goodrich.*

Fox took the book and held it close to his face, nose wrinkling, mouth ajar. I nudged him to let him know I couldn't see. He lowered the journal and together we read paragraphs of notes about Point Pleasant, with eyewitness accounts of Mothman sightings, dates and times and locations, all in the same small, neat handwriting. Halfway through the book, the focus switched to Clark. Sightings were less frequent, eyewitnesses reluctant to talk. *Why so many sightings in Point Pleasant?* I wondered. And if he liked to show up where the next disaster was due to strike, why hadn't other people seen him in Athens?

"All these sightings," I said. "Do you think he's actually causing the disasters?"

"Don't know," he murmured, engrossed in his reading. "Makes sense, though."

I rested my chin in my hand, lost in thought.

On the last page of the book, a single phrase jumped out at me: *I must save my Nora.* I frowned. Save her from what? The landslide? Hadn't they been working together to stop it?

It made me feel fragile, like bad things would find you no matter how careful you were. But I knew we had to move on. As interesting as the journal was, it didn't provide much help. We still had little clue what we were supposed to stop, or how, or what would happen if we didn't except that people would likely die.

And we were running out of time.

I set the journal aside.

Fox used his phone to look up Monday's event schedule for the Field House while I fired up Dad's laptop.

Though I didn't have Fox's people skills, I did know a thing or two about computers.

I started by checking theater costume sites for clothing styles like the ones I'd seen in my vision. The nearest I could pin it down was sometime in the late 1800s.

I looked for records of Edgars, Elsies, and Williams in Ohio, Kentucky, and West Virginia from the 1880s onward, but without last names or a specific town it was all but impossible, until I added the word *murder*. Within minutes I pulled up a scanned newspaper article from Ravenswood, West Virginia, in July 1879, reporting the death of William Bennett by gunshot wound. The weapon was fired by longtime friend Edgar Tripp, who disappeared without a trace. William was survived by his fiancée, Elsie Archer.

It was real. All of it. I shuddered, thinking again of my vision and the look in Edgar's eyes when he'd pulled that trigger.

At least now we had a place to start.

Finally we decided to call it a night. Mason had fallen asleep on the rug, clutching his roll of duct tape. I shook him awake and sent him off to bed.

Fox and I didn't talk much. We said good-night to Aunt Barb and Uncle Bill before plodding upstairs, knowing we were in over our heads.

I carted the journals and shadow box up to my room and set them on my desk. I was afraid to keep the pin too close or too far away, so I settled for placing it on my bedside table, as far away as possible from Momma's picture.

Climbing into bed, I realized I had school the next day. I sighed. It seemed like such a waste of time.

I wanted to call Dad, but Aunt Barb had said he was resting, trying to get better. Tomorrow I would remind her about her promise that we could go see him. But tonight . . . I knew he had his cell phone with him. He was probably asleep. I sent him a text anyway:

Hi Dad. How r u?

I waited ten minutes with no response. Maybe he had his phone turned off. Maybe he wasn't allowed to use it in the hospital. I stared at the screen, willing it to light up.

Finally my text alert pinged. I grabbed the phone.

Hi Josie Bug

How r u? Miss you.
Wanted 2 come c u today.

Miss you too. Tired. Bored.

When do u come home?

Few more days

Need anything?

Cheeseburger?

I would if I could

We texted back and forth for a few more minutes before saying good-night. I held the phone tightly, wanting
desperately to hug him for real.

I stared at the shadow box on my desk. Was it John's?
Was it just a coincidence that he collected bugs, or did
the fascination start after he found out about the curse?

Either way, the thing was creepy as sin. The moths
looked like they could crawl out from under the glass at
any moment and start flying at me with their scratchy

brown wings. I tried setting a stack of papers on top of it so I wouldn't have to look at it. Every few minutes I glanced over at it anyway. It was just as hideous every single time.

Finally I tumbled out of bed. I grabbed the shadow box, hurried into the hall, and stuffed it deep down into a clothes hamper.

I switched off my light and burrowed down under the covers. As I drifted off to sleep, the phrase from John's journal haunted me: *I must save my Nora.*

Did John know she would die in the landslide? Why wasn't he with her?

Why couldn't he save her?

10

WHEN I OPENED MY EYES THE NEXT morning, the pin was the first thing I saw. The picture of Momma was the second. She smiled at me like she always did, with laughing eyes and rosy cheeks and a kind face. I sat up in a panic. I'd forgotten to kiss her picture good night. I hadn't missed a morning or evening since she died. It felt like a betrayal, and a bad omen besides. I picked up the photo and kissed it twice for good measure.

Fox barged in around six forty-five and tossed the shadow box on my bed. "Aunt Barb found this in the hamper. You might want to put it somewhere safe."

I made a face. "Thanks."

"Don't worry," he said, clapping me on the shoulder. "I think it's creepy, too. I would have done the same thing."

We begged to skip school again so we could visit Dad. Aunt Barb was having none of it.

"But we haven't seen him since Monday," Fox said.

"You've missed too many days already."

"But next week is spring break!" I said. "It's not like we're doing anything important in class this week anyway."

She stood firm. "After school," she said, and the conversation was over.

School dragged by, minute by agonizing minute. Three of my teachers caught me staring out the window. They were sympathetic, but I could feel the other kids' eyes on me, curious. I didn't want the attention or the sympathy. I just wanted to be with Dad.

* * *

I gladly left it all behind when Aunt Barb picked me up at the end of the day. We drove from the middle school to the grade school to grab the boys, then made our way to the hospital. I insisted we stop on the way to get Dad a cheeseburger.

But Dad's room was quiet and dark when we got there. His face was too pale, his body too still, tucked under a scratchy blanket that made me itch just looking at it. A nurse was writing something on a chart at the foot of his bed.

Aunt Barb whispered for us to wait in the hall. She talked with the nurse for a couple of minutes while we stood there watching, afraid to meet one another's eyes. A fretful silence settled over us, the scene not so different from our last few visits with Momma.

Finally Aunt Barb returned. She led us to a bank of chairs at the end of the hall. "Your daddy's had an allergic reaction to his antibiotics, so they've had to change his medication."

We blinked back at her.

"He's running a fever. They think it's better if we try again tomorrow."

Tears brimmed in Mason's eyes. Fox's face went all still, like that day at the Goodrich house when Dad fell. The cheeseburger sat cooling in its paper bag, a grease stain spreading along the bottom.

Aunt Barb slipped one arm around Mason, the other around Fox. "Come on. No more frowns. Let's get some ice cream at the cafeteria. By tomorrow your dad will be fussing and trying to bribe the nurses to let him leave."

I caught Mason watching me closely, so I pasted on a phony smile and tickled the back of his neck. "Bet I can eat more ice cream than you," I told him.

"Can not!"

"Can so!"

I thought Fox might refuse to play along, but he wasn't about to be upstaged. "I get all the sprinkles," he said, fast-walking ahead of Mason.

"Fox!" Mason shouted, doubling his steps to keep up.

I glanced at Aunt Barb. She reached out to squeeze my hand. "You're a good girl, Josie Fletcher." I felt my cheeks grow warm. "I'd say something to Fox," she whispered, "but his head's big enough already, don't you think?"

I laughed. I'd almost forgotten what it felt like.

* * *

"So there's a quilt show at the Field House during the day on Monday, and the state high school basketball championship game that night," Fox said. "That means a ton of people."

My worry rose another notch. "That complicates things."

After our disappointing visit to the hospital, Fox and I had retreated to the Cave to work on what we'd started calling our Disaster Avoidance Plan.

I began spreading across the table a stack of papers that I'd printed out the day before, taping them down one by one.

"What are those?" Fox said.

"Blueprints for the Field House."

"Where did you get them?"

I shrugged. "You'd be surprised what you can find online."

"Huh."

"So," I said, standing back to study the blueprints. "How do we keep all those people away?"

"We call in an anonymous tip, get them to evacuate the building. But it has to be credible," Fox said.

"Could we say there's a bomb?"

"That might do it, although if they trace it back to us we'd be in massive amounts of trouble. Even making a threat is like a federal crime or something."

"Let's call that a last resort," I said. "What else?"

"I thought of something," he said with a crooked grin, "but you won't like it much."

"Tell me."

"We burn down the building Sunday night. Then

nobody can be in it on Monday whenever the disaster strikes."

"You're right. I hate it. Next?"

His gaze shifted sideways. "I'm working on it, okay? Feel free to chime in with any plans of your own."

"The problem is we have no idea what kind of disaster we're supposed to stop or what time of day it's supposed to happen," I said, pacing. "I wonder if John knew. I wish we could talk to him."

A knock at the door caught us by surprise. Uncle Bill swung the door open and poked his head inside. He whistled when he caught sight of the broken window, which we'd covered over with garbage bags and duct tape to keep out the worst of the cold. Luckily we'd already swept away the chalk scribbles with a push broom.

He didn't ask about the window, though. He just scratched the back of his neck and said, "Fox, your dad wants you to call Saturday's auction. He thinks you're ready, and so do I. We could sure use the extra help."

Fox's smile made the whole room seem brighter. "Really?"

Uncle Bill nodded. "You'll want to get some practice in before Saturday." He gave a sort of half wave and let himself out.

"Wow." Fox's happy mood lasted for all of three

seconds. His smile disappeared when he glanced at the papers taped to the table. "Oh. I guess this is kind of more important, huh?"

The past several days had taken their toll. Both of us were anxious and low on sleep. We'd all but forgotten our plan to go to the state fair. We'd pretty much forgotten about *anything* simple or fun.

I took his arm and led him out of the Cave, shutting the door behind me. Dusk was already starting to creep across the sky. We had only a few hours left before bed. "Go and practice, just for an hour or so. You've been waiting for this for a long time. I'll keep researching and let you know if I find anything. It'll be fine."

His brows scrunched together, his expression doubtful. "Josie."

"Go on. All we have to do is figure out how to keep people away from the Field House on Monday. It's not like it's a landslide or a faulty bridge. It's just a building. We're Fletchers. We'll get it done."

Fox did something then that he never, ever did—at least not since Momma died.

He hugged me.

I stood utterly still, overcome by shock. "Thanks, Josie. One hour, then I'm right back in this, okay?"

He ran for the house as I continued to stand there, wondering what other surprises the day might bring.

* * *

I claimed Dad's study so I could use the computer. I could hear Fox upstairs practicing his calling skills behind his closed bedroom door, smooth voice rushing along like a bubbling stream. I tried to feel happy for him as I read about one terrible disaster after another.

I started in Ohio, then moved on to Kentucky, Indiana, and West Virginia, searching all the way back to 1880. From what we knew so far, wherever Mothman appeared, disaster followed. I read about collapsed mines and sunken riverboats; about plane crashes and fifty-car pileups; about floods, and fires, and hundred-year blizzards. I sat with a notebook open in front of me, mapping out a time line to find some connection between the disasters, some way to tell if Mothman had played a role. After a while I realized there were tears dripping from my cheeks to the notebook page, making the ink spread in splotchy circles.

Dad's chair squeaked as I leaned my head back and rubbed at my eyes. Sadness gripped me, so thick and heavy it made my whole body ache. The stories were all so awful. I couldn't let something like that happen in Athens—I just couldn't.

I found myself wishing our ghost was there, just so I'd have some company. How twisted was that? But he understood. He knew things I needed to know. He'd lived through one disaster and was still trying to stop another, even in death.

"Mr. Goodrich?" I whispered. I wasn't quite ready to put the pin back on yet, afraid I'd get caught up in another vision. But I wondered if he was nearby, if he could hear me. "John? I could really use some help, if you have any suggestions."

A chilly gust of air curled up from the floor and swept across the desk, scattering the papers piled there. I scrambled to catch them as they fluttered to the floor. As I shuffled the stacks around, trying to make everything look like it did before I got there, I spotted a manila envelope with Dad's name on it and the word *Goodrich* printed in block letters.

It had already been opened, so I didn't hesitate. I tipped the envelope, and a letter slid into my waiting hand:

> Mr. Fletcher,
>
> I'm writing on behalf of my client, John Goodrich. John passed away yesterday afternoon. He left strict instructions that you be the one to handle his estate in the event of his death. I know you spoke with him at length just this week, and I believe the terms you discussed align with what I've summarized below.
>
> A contract is being written up with

details of payment for your services. You can expect to receive your standard 30 percent fee of the proceeds, and are invited to select any pieces from the estate that you may wish for your personal collection. The remaining funds are to be used to create a disaster relief fund for the city of Athens.

You undoubtedly know some of the history behind the Clark landslide, although I don't believe you knew John personally. I request that this matter be handled in the strictest of confidence. The details of John's death, specifically, will create quite a stir when they come out, so I will tell you now that John took his own life. As you know, he was terminally ill, and it seems the long years of pain and grief finally took their toll. An autopsy will be performed to confirm this, but I received a letter from him by courier that same day, making his intentions clear and spelling out his last wishes in detail. Once word of the suicide gets out, both the public and the media will show no mercy in uncovering every gruesome detail.

John left items in the bedroom safe for your eyes alone. I do not have the combination, but I'm sure you have connections to assist you with that.

You may expect the contract to arrive by courier in the next few days. Thank you for your assistance and your discretion.

Sincerely,
Robert Latimer

I read the letter twice more, staring at the word *suicide* in anger and disbelief.

"Is it true?" I said aloud to the empty room. "You killed yourself? You dumped this curse on our family because you couldn't handle it anymore—is that it?"

I picked up the nearest pile of papers and threw them. Had he really given up? He'd lived in that house for forty years, waiting for some disaster he was supposed to stop, then killed himself a few weeks before it was supposed to happen? It didn't make sense.

I had no idea how to prevent a disaster or end some mysterious curse.

I felt scared, and furious, and more alone than I could ever remember. So I did what I knew Momma would do.

I kept looking.

II

THURSDAY AND FRIDAY FLEW BY IN A BLUR of school, auction preparations, and research. My teachers were no longer taking it easy on me, and with Dad gone, we all had to shoulder the extra work.

Fox took the news about John's suicide much better than I did. He arched an eyebrow in surprise and went back to perfecting his calling skills. He still tried to help where he could, but I knew the auction had claimed the bulk of his attention. I just hoped I'd get it back when the auction was over.

On Thursday, Dad felt up to talking on the phone, and on Friday, we spent almost an hour at the hospital with him awake and sitting up and everything. He was still so tired, though. I ached for him to be his indestructible self again, to leap out of bed and make everything okay. He stayed awake long enough to insist that we quit fussing over him, and to give Fox some last-minute coaching on calling the auction. I could see that Dad was proud of Fox, who soaked up every word, his face at once solemn and eager.

I pretended not to feel the twinge of jealousy that zinged through me as I waited for my turn to say goodbye.

* * *

My research dug up plenty of newspaper articles scattered across the last hundred-plus years about sightings of a part man, part moth—more than I'd expected. They were almost always buried on the back page, the paper going out of its way to make the witness look like a raving fool. None of the encounters came close to the level of notoriety reached in Point Pleasant. After a man named John Keel wrote a book about the sightings there, Mothman went mainstream, earning his spot in the monster Hall of Fame.

Still, many times the sightings were concentrated in a particular town, and when I searched those towns for disasters, I almost always found one, including an 1886 train derailment in Ravenswood, the town where Elsie had lived.

But my best find was a page-long interview in 1902 with a politician named Benjamin Park, who was running for city council. He said he'd been singled out to warn his town of a looming disaster, though he couldn't say what kind. Jacob Jeffreys, a friend of the family, had died in a nearby town trying to prevent another disaster, and had provided Benjamin with a powerful, mystical method of divining where tragedy would strike next. Mothman wasn't mentioned, but the article said that if elected, Benjamin claimed he "would have more influence to avert certain doom."

In the photograph of Mr. Park, I could see a tiny gleam of gold at his collar. I grabbed a magnifying glass for a closer look. Sure enough, he was wearing the moth pin.

Further reading revealed that Benjamin Park lost the election, and twelve people died when a mine collapsed a few weeks later.

I worked up the courage to try on the pin again, more than once, but nothing happened. I didn't even see John's ghost. I wondered if he stayed away because he felt guilty about the suicide.

* * *

Our Saturday morning started at 4:30 a.m. By the time most kids were just waking up, Fox, Mason, and I were already exhausted from hours of fetching and carrying.

People started lining up outside the auction building before dawn for the eight o'clock preview. By 6:00 a.m. the line snaked all the way down one wall and around the corner.

Aunt Barb, face flushed and sweat already dampening

her shirt, bustled about in a state of near hysteria, as Mitch and Uncle Bill wrestled a few last-minute furniture pieces into place.

Fox paced back and forth in front of the podium, trying out auctioneer voices.

The only one who seemed to be enjoying himself was Mason. He ran from the storeroom to the auction floor to the office to the bank of windows where he could gawk at the gathering crowd outside. I couldn't help but smile as I watched him.

My smile faded as I felt the weight of the moth pin near my collarbone. I'd changed my mind a dozen times that morning about whether to wear it. In the end, I fastened it to my T-shirt and covered it up with a sweater to avoid any questions.

At eight o'clock, Uncle Bill opened the doors.

The morning had dawned cool and foggy, a fine drizzle seeping into the clothes and hair of all those waiting customers, adding to the overall restlessness. I recognized all our regulars, but there were many, many more faces I was seeing for the first time. People from neighboring towns in all directions had come to gawk, or maybe to be part of something that didn't happen often: the life of a local legend on display for all to see.

I thought of John's sad eyes and bowed shoulders, and

even though I was mad at him, I suddenly wished I could send all the gawkers away. They crowded around the tables, handling and pawing every piece, jostling one another for position. I realized I actually *wanted* to see John again, mostly because I felt like he owed me an explanation for what he'd done.

I ducked into the storeroom and closed the door behind me. By the end of the weekend, it would be filled with someone else's possessions, but at the moment it was blessedly empty.

I took a long, slow breath, soaking in the quiet. When I opened my eyes, John was there beside me.

I startled and clutched my chest. He moved back a few feet to give me some space.

Save them, he mouthed, and even though I couldn't hear the words I understood them well enough.

"I'm trying. But I have to know why you killed yourself. I deserve to know."

He glanced over his shoulder. I followed his gaze and saw . . . a woman.

A ghost. She was tall and thin, with limp hair and a pinched face.

Nora, I realized with sudden clarity. I recognized her from the photo albums.

"Mrs. Goodrich?" I whispered.

She blinked at me, her face twisted in torment. She

was just as we'd seen her in the albums, except now she was drained of all color like John. Her image flickered in and out, like a dying streetlight.

"You want to free her?" I said to John. "Is she still trapped by the curse?"

John nodded.

"Are there others who have been cursed over the years? Are they trapped, too?"

He nodded again.

"So if we stop this disaster, then the curse is broken and you can be together, at peace?"

One more nod confirmed my hunch. John glanced again at his wife, then back at me.

My eyes filled. My throat burned. I felt so sorry for them. I had to help, even though I still hadn't figured out *how*.

"Josie?" Fox poked his head into the room. "There you are! Quit wasting time and get out here. Aunt Barb needs help handing out numbers."

"Coming." I kept my back to him so I could swipe at a couple of stray tears.

When I looked up again, John and Nora were gone.

I left the pin on in case they came back.

The crowd had mushroomed even more and was still growing. People had already claimed all the seats and were now lining up against the back wall. The rest spilled out through the garage-sized doorway, the sliding door left open to accommodate them.

I shuffled and squeezed my way into the office to help Aunt Barb hand out bid cards, recording bidders' names and addresses and collecting five dollars per head, making change, and answering endless questions.

"Got any maps for sale today?" said a sweet Southern voice. I squinted through the plexiglass window to see Amelia, wearing the same visor and fanny pack.

"Hi there!" Her whole face smiled. "Josie, right?"

"Yes. Hi! Still in town, I see."

"Oh yes. Couldn't miss this one. How's that new camera of yours working out?"

I'd forgotten all about it, our sixty-dollar investment lying in the Dumpster in a dozen pieces. And I could see John just fine without it now. Had it been only a week ago? It seemed like a lifetime.

"It's great," I said, and changed the subject. "You got your eye on anything special today?"

She frowned. "Not yet. So many rubberneckers here this morning." She giggled. "Guess I'm one of them."

"Well, good luck to you," I said, glad to see a friendly face, wishing we could talk longer but well aware of the twenty people in line behind her still waiting to be helped.

The auction started at nine thirty sharp. As usual, Uncle Bill served as spokesmodel and Aunt Barb manned the logbook. But this week, it was Fox who stood at the podium, beaming at the crowd. He'd agonized over what to wear, finally settling on the dress shirt and tie Aunt Barb had bought for him to wear to church on Christmas Eve.

Fox put every ounce of his charm and humor on display. His voice galloped and coaxed, baiting, chiding, getting those bids up when they faltered, using every tool in his toolbox to sway the crowd.

I had the unglamorous job of runner: if items were portable enough, I'd run over and hand them to the winning bidder as soon as the bidding ended. Then the buyers settled up what they owed once the auction was over. I stayed so busy I didn't have time to keep an eye out for John and Nora.

Finally I got the chance for a quick breather. I found an empty spot of wall at the back of the room and leaned against it with a sigh. A conversation nearby interrupted my thoughts. Two old women were carrying on in overloud whispers. "Did you see this morning's article about John Goodrich?" I leaned closer as casually as I could.

"The autopsy report said he didn't die of natural causes."

"Don't tell me they suspect foul play."

"Worse. They think it might have been a suicide."

All other sound and motion faded from my notice as I zeroed in on the conversation, trying to learn anything new. I scanned the room and found John hovering just behind Fox's shoulder. He gave a single nod in my direction, meeting my gaze over the heads of the crowd. The suicide was a crucial detail, I could tell, but I didn't know *why*.

Suddenly a look of fear crossed his face. He vanished.

The lights far above us flickered off and then on, then

stayed off. Sunlight still streamed in through the open sliding door, but murmurs of unease crept through the crowd.

"Now, now, folks," Fox said. "There's nothing to worry about. Just a minor—"

Someone screamed.

Red eyes glowed from high in one corner of the room, up near the ceiling. The shadowed outline of a winged figure hovered there.

Another person screamed, and another. Chairs scraped the floor as people got to their feet. Panicked murmurs spread, voices rising.

"What is it?"

"What's happening?"

"Is it real?"

Uncle Bill took the microphone from Fox. "People!" His amplified voice filled the room. Fox banged the gavel on the podium several times. It seemed to quiet the crowd for a few seconds, until, with a great swell of air and a mighty flapping, the creature swooped low over the crowd, crossing to the opposite corner.

More screams erupted. Feet thundered as people shoved their way toward the exit. I was swept along with the rest, fighting just to stay standing. People rushed toward the big square of light like it was salvation itself.

I found myself outside without knowing how I got there, glad I was still in one piece.

A tiny old woman stumbled on the threshold of the doorway as more customers streamed out; I quickly grabbed her arm and pulled her to one side before she could fall and be trampled.

"Thank you, dear," she breathed, her hand to her chest.

The crowd gasped and looked to the heavens as Mothman whooshed out of the building and into the bright sky, a dark stain against brilliant blue.

"Mothman!"

"It's Mothman. He's returned!"

Finally, Fox, Mason, Uncle Bill, and Aunt Barb made it out of the building, the last few, just in time to catch sight of Mothman as he looped around for another low pass over the crowd.

People were screaming, crying, and taking pictures with their cell phones. I watched my family as recognition dawned on their faces—along with a healthy dose of horror.

"What in the name of heaven and earth is that creature doing here?" Aunt Barb shouted. She had scooped Mason up and he clung to her, his arms around her neck. When he saw me, he squirmed in her grasp and reached for me. I rubbed his back but left him where he was.

Most in the crowd were still occupied with Mothman's show, but a few spotted Uncle Bill and pounced, ranting about publicity stunts and tasteless pranks.

Even with his eyes glued to the skies, Fox found me, gavel hanging from one hand, forgotten. He whistled long and low. "It's really him. What's he doing here? Why now?"

I swallowed. "I don't know." In a way it was a relief to know we weren't crazy, that we hadn't dreamed up the whole thing. But the sight of Mothman also filled me with dread. He was the most terrifying thing I'd ever seen. "Do you think he's trying to distract us from stopping the disaster?"

Fox was too preoccupied to answer. Confusion grew as people tried to either get to safety or find a better vantage point. Frantic customers ran every which way, calling for friends or family members. One crashed into Fox's shoulder and almost knocked him over. Another stepped on my foot as he stumbled past. Fear rippled through the crowd like a wave.

Suddenly I sensed a figure move to stand beside me, uncomfortably close. Just as I realized it was John Goodrich, several things happened in rapid progression:

Mothman lurched down and stopped in the air just above us, his gaze fixed on John, crimson eyes burning with hatred.

John's image cringed and flickered, but he returned the stare, chin lifted, jaw set in anger.

Mothman stretched out one bony finger and pointed . . . at me. Though there was only a dark void where his mouth should be, I *felt* a grin twist his features. I shrank back, numb with fright. The pin burned cold against my skin.

John raised his arms as if to shield me.

Then I watched Mothman's gaze slowly shift to study my family one by one.

He turned to survey the chaos of the crowd, nodding once as if pleased, his coal-black robes fluttering in the breeze.

And then, with one final swoop, he soared high into the air and disappeared.

THE POWER BLINKED BACK ON INSIDE THE auction building.

The world around me came into focus again. My heart raced. The pin pulsed with energy, bitterly cold.

John was nowhere in sight.

Fox stepped close to me, our shoulders touching. Mason wriggled free of Aunt Barb's grasp so he could grab my hand and hold on. We'd all felt the weight of Mothman's stare, the reality that for whatever reason, he'd set the Fletchers in his sights.

Aunt Barb and Uncle Bill stood huddled in conversation as the crowd grew more and more restless. Truthfully, Uncle Bill listened while Aunt Barb did all the talking.

Poor Uncle Bill shied away from drama of any kind. If it was up to him, he would march back inside, continue the auction, and pretend none of this had ever happened. But he and Aunt Barb were trapped in the thick of the unhappy crowd, some pointing fingers and shouting accusations of a hoax, others hysterical and carrying on about impending doom.

It didn't seem to matter that several people got in their cars and left right away, because more showed up in their place. The crowd swelled as reporters and TV trucks and hundreds of locals flocked to our property.

* * *

After Uncle Bill and Aunt Barb insisted a hundred times over that it wasn't a stunt, people generally agreed that what they'd seen was real. With that many witnesses and the clean light of day as a backdrop, Mothman would've been awfully hard to fake. Plus the locals knew our family. So we didn't get the blame, just lots and lots and *lots* more questions.

People wanted to know if we'd seen Mothman before today. Had he ever spoken to us, and if so, what did he say? Did we have any idea where he came from, or what he wanted? Had we ever been to Point Pleasant? Had we seen the movie? Were we going to reschedule the auction, or shut the business down altogether? Was Jim Fletcher still in the hospital, and how was he doing, and when was he expected home? How would he react to the news? Did we plan to sell our story to CNN, or maybe the Syfy network?

On and on it went, with no end in sight.

I pulled Fox aside and whispered, "With all these cameras here, maybe we should try to warn people about the Field House."

"What are we supposed to say? That the ghost of John Goodrich told us there would be some kind of a disaster on Monday? It sounds crazy. People barely believe that we didn't fake this whole thing. I don't think we should give them any more reasons to call us liars."

"But we'll never get a better chance—"

A smiling woman wearing too much makeup interrupted, stepping between us and pushing a microphone in my face.

"Hi there, young lady. Molly Madigan with Channel Three News. I was told you're one of the Fletchers, that your family owns the auction house."

"Uh, yes. Yes, I am. We do. Hi."

Another reporter with her own microphone and cameraman glommed onto Fox and hustled him off to one side. I saw him trying to fix his hair with his fingers.

"And can you tell us your name?"

"Huh?" My attention returned to the reporter beside me. The camera was right there, staring at me like a big black eye. "Uh . . . Josie."

"Okay, Josie. Can you tell me how you felt when you first saw the moth creature? Were you scared?"

I thought about the first time I'd actually seen those red eyes and could truthfully answer: "Y-yes."

"Why do you think he's here now? Do you think he's trying to tell us something?"

"I—uh." I stumbled over what to say, realizing Fox was right about us sounding crazy. "He, uh, he was at Point Pleasant, right? He, like, warns people about disasters, doesn't he?"

"That's what the stories say. Now, I understand you lost your mother a few years back. Are you worried the rest of your family might be next? What do you think your mother would say if she knew you had all been marked for death?"

I glanced around, trying to find anyone wearing an expression like the sucker-punch surprise and fury I felt at her horrible question. But everyone listening in just nodded, waiting for an answer.

I looked right at the camera. "I think, if my mother were here right now . . ."

"Yes?"

"She'd kick your skinny little butt halfway to Cleveland for your terrible manners."

I turned my back and stomped away, the lovely image of her shocked, fake-pretty face etched forever in my head.

Fear, worry, and anger all churned around inside me. I slipped into the house, soaking up the quiet after the chaos outside. The noise of the crowd was muffled enough that I could hear the refrigerator humming. The bathroom faucet dripped. Birds chirped and cheeped outside the window. I could almost pretend nothing was wrong until the pin pulsed like a heartbeat, still painfully cold.

"John?" I whispered, but he wasn't there. I even took the pin off and put it back on again.

Nothing.

I slumped at the kitchen table. My stomach rumbled. Lunchtime had long come and gone.

I called and ordered a couple of pizzas with Dad's credit card number, which we kept on a Post-it note inside the kitchen cupboard for emergencies. I decided that a Mothman sighting counted as an emergency.

Fox and Mason joined me a few minutes later. They

sat down at the table without a word. I couldn't think of anything to say, so I grabbed a jar of peanut butter and a sleeve of crackers from the pantry. Even cursed people had to eat.

We sat munching in silence, staring with fascination at the crumbs we were leaving in the peanut butter jar. I focused on breathing in and out, in and out.

Eventually Aunt Barb and Uncle Bill shuffled in. They stood there in the kitchen like they'd never seen it before, like they were in the wrong house, the wrong life. I offered them a chair and told them pizza was on the way. Uncle Bill chose to stand, fussing with his hat. Aunt Barb stood, too, looking us over. "How are you all holding up?"

Nobody answered.

"That good, huh?" She flashed a tired smile. "Listen, we will solve this, all right? No silly bug man is going to get the better of us, you hear me?"

We nodded.

"Do you think he'll come back?" Mason whispered.

"I don't know, sugar." She brushed a few stray cracker crumbs from Mason's face. "Seems to me he's a bully, though. All bluster. Hey, Mason, why don't you let me talk to your brother and sister for a minute, okay?" she said. "You want to watch some TV?" He nodded and trotted into the living room.

I wondered if it was time to come clean with everything we knew. From the look on his face, I guessed Fox was wondering the same thing.

Before I could decide, Mason bellowed, "Uncle Bill! You're on TV!"

We all rushed into the living room, where video footage of Mothman played over and over under the heading *Breaking News.* They cut to interviews with several of our customers and neighbors, and then Uncle Bill popped up on the screen.

"You look good, dear," Aunt Barb said. "The gray in your hair—it's distinguished. Don't you think so, Josie?"

"Aunt Barb! I think all of this is insane—that's what I think. Don't you even want to know why Mothman is here, why he showed up at our auction? Maybe we should be worrying about that!"

She flinched. I felt awful for yelling. I knew she was doing the best she could, but I couldn't help wishing that Dad were here instead. Or Momma. "Sorry," I mumbled.

"No, I'm sorry, honey. You're right. Of course you're right. I'm just a little off-kilter right now. Ever since we took on that Goodrich estate, things have been so upside down." She sniffed and dabbed at her eyes.

Uncle Bill slipped an arm around her shoulders. "Mason, turn that thing off, huh?"

Aunt Barb looked down at her rumpled clothes,

patted her unruly hair. "I must look a fright. Will you three be all right if we take a few minutes to get cleaned up?"

"Sure," I said. "We'll wait for the pizza."

She and Uncle Bill headed out to their place over the garage.

Mason went to the front window. "What are all those people still doing out there?"

I moved the curtains aside to peer out at the cow pasture just beyond our property line. Seven more news trucks had joined the first two. Hundreds of people had set up lawn chairs, tents, and blankets, like they were waiting for a fireworks show.

Fox joined us at the window. "They want to catch a glimpse of Mothman. Be a part of history."

"Who would *want* to see him?" Mason said.

"People who don't know any better," Fox said.

Many of the bystanders carried signs or watched the sky, looking worried. But others acted like it was all a big party. Somebody had a grill fired up and was turning hot dogs as they sizzled. Others were slapping a beach ball as it skimmed over the heads of the gathered crowd.

Unbelievable.

"I'm going for a walk," I said suddenly.

"Right now? Alone?" Fox said.

"I just need to clear my head. I won't be long."

He glanced at Mason, who clung to Fox's sleeve with all ten fingers. "Just . . . be careful, okay?"

I nodded. Grabbing my coat, I left the house and started walking, heading away from the circus our lives had become. The afternoon sun shone down, surprisingly warm. I followed the road, sticking close to the shoulder, but there weren't many cars to avoid. They were all coming from town in the opposite direction, so I had the road pretty much to myself.

Until I felt a prickle on the back of my neck.

I looked over my shoulder to find John trailing me. My hand flew to my collar. I was still wearing the moth pin.

He kept about five feet between us. He wasn't walking, exactly. That is, his legs weren't moving, and he didn't really float, either. His image would just wink out, then wink back in the next second a few feet closer than before.

I sighed and kept walking. I could always take the pin off, but for all I knew he'd still be there, out of sight. For some reason, I found that even more unsettling. I turned around and walked backward so I could see him.

"Why'd you do it, John?" I asked out loud. "How could you take your own life? The letter from the lawyer said you had a terminal illness. Was that it? You got tired of being sick?"

He shook his head. *No.*

"Good. Because my mom was sick for a long time, and it was awful, but she still fought up until the end. So what was it? Were you trying to break the curse?"

A nod. *Yes.*

"Well, guess what? It didn't work. Do you realize what you've done to us?"

He hung his head. I rolled my eyes. I would *not* feel sorry for a ghost—no, sir.

Then he looked up. Purpose had replaced his usual sadness. *Save them*, he mouthed.

"Is that all we have to do to end the curse?" I said. "Then everything will be okay?"

He looked away.

I stopped walking. "John? Please, you have to help me figure this out."

But he flickered and disappeared.

"John!" I turned in a slow circle, but there was no sign of him. I trudged back to the house, more confused and anxious than ever.

I found Fox and Mason still staring out the window, eating pizza. I could hear Aunt Barb on the phone, her voice climbing and falling like the cars on a roller coaster. At this rate she'd probably be on the phone for the rest of her life. I thought about Dad and how worried he must be if he'd seen the news. I vowed to call him, just to check in and let him know we were okay.

"What are you guys doing?"

"All those people," Fox was saying. "Think of how many ghost maps we could sell. Or bottled water, even. We could make a fortune! Josie, you could print out some more of those maps, right?"

I glared at him. "Really? Is that all you can think about? No, I will not print any more of those stupid maps, you selfish, greedy *infant*."

"Whoa, what's the problem?"

I dragged him into the kitchen, struggling to keep my voice at a whisper. "The *problem*, since you've obviously forgotten, is that in two days a whole bunch of people are going to die, and the freaking Mothman just showed up at our auction, and you want to sell bottled water like it's a sporting event! We have to figure out a way to keep people away from the Field House."

"I wasn't being serious. Sheesh. I was trying to distract our little brother. Besides, I already thought of something," he said, easy as you please.

"What? You mind sharing this brilliant idea with me?"

"Simple. We play Mothman—draw people's attention to the Field House and away from our front yard. We leave messages warning people about the disaster and make it seem like they're from Mothman. It'll make the news and people will listen because they're already waiting for his next move, practically begging for it."

"What kind of messages? How do we fake something like that?"

"Spray paint."

"That's illegal."

"Do you want to save those people or not?"

I remained stubborn, not wanting to admit it was a pretty good idea. "And you just thought of this while you were plotting how to make money off those people?"

"Sure. We'll just have to iron out the details. What do you think, Josie? Think it'll work?"

It was a classic Fox move, deflecting anger by asking for my opinion, and dang if it didn't work every time. He looked nothing but totally sincere, and it was maddening.

"Fine. But we should focus on the university, right around the Field House. And we'll have to wait until after dark so we don't get caught. How do we get there? What do we tell Aunt Barb?"

Fox smiled. "Leave that to me."

W E PUT OUR PLAN INTO ACTION THAT very night. It was simple—even kind of stupid, really.

Fox and I each stuffed a backpack with cans of red spray paint—auction leftovers that had been piling up in the garage for years. Fox even managed to squeeze in a roller brush and a collapsible extension pole.

Next we dug through the Halloween boxes and found two pairs of novelty goggles with red light-up eyes. Add some AA batteries and—presto—instant Mothman.

Step three was trickier: convincing Aunt Barb to let us out of the house after dark.

We started by pushing to reschedule the auction. It helped that Aunt Barb and Uncle Bill wanted the Goodrich stuff gone as soon as possible. Sunday and Monday were out of the question, since Fox and I had a disaster to stop and only two more days to do it. Plus Dad would hopefully be home Monday or Tuesday and would need time to settle in, so Wednesday seemed like the earliest reasonable day. We couldn't come right out and say that, though, so I printed up flyers advertising Wednesday as the new auction date and presented them to Uncle Bill. He looked them over and slowly nodded his approval, no doubt glad for one less thing to handle.

Since Mitch was still outside trying to get people to go home, Fox mentioned that maybe Mitch's time would be better spent dropping off the flyers at local businesses.

Uncle Bill seemed to like that idea, too. But Fox and I insisted that Mitch couldn't go out on an empty stomach, and shouldn't he stay for dinner?

Aunt Barb never passed up a chance to cook. She started pulling food from the fridge and pans from the cupboard to whip up her famous fried chicken.

The whole time she was cooking, Fox and I hung around the kitchen, getting in her way. When Barb put us to work coating chicken or peeling potatoes, we complained, and moped, and did such a sorry job that she banned us from her sight until dinnertime.

After we ate and Mitch was getting set to leave, Fox asked, "Can Josie and I ride along with him?"

"I don't know," Aunt Barb said. "It's getting late."

"But we're so booooooored," Fox said.

"I guess we could stay to help clean up the kitchen," I said.

Barb all but pushed us out the door. "No, no, I'll get Mason to help me. You two run along and help Mitch. You could probably use the break."

Fox hid a sly smile.

So far, so good.

* * *

Once we were on the road, we started in on Mitch. After several stops around town, we had him convinced that Dad always put up flyers at Ohio University.

I nearly cheered when he pointed the car toward campus.

"Boy, that was some crazy day today," Mitch said on the drive there, shaking his head. "The stuff that people believe."

"What . . . uh, what do you mean?" Fox said.

"Well, you know. All those people thinking they saw Mothman."

Fox and I exchanged confused glances.

"What did you see, Mitch?" I asked.

"Looked like some kind of endangered bird escaped from the zoo," he said, scratching his head. "Don't know how it ended up in your auction house, though."

Fox fake-chuckled. "You're right. That was crazy, wasn't it? Mothman. *Pffttt.* I guess people see what they want to see, don't they?"

"Darn straight." Mitch parked in a lot across from the Field House, a high-traffic corner of the campus near the West Green residence halls. Stars dotted the night sky.

"Stay close, guys," he said as we climbed out of the car. "This is a big place."

"Maybe we should just wait here," Fox said. "We don't want to slow you down."

"Oh, no, I don't think that's such a good idea."

Fox nudged me. "Josie told me she wasn't feeling well, right, Josie? She didn't want me to say anything, but . . ."

Mitch looked at me. "Is that true?"

I rubbed my stomach. "It's probably no big deal, just too much fried chicken."

"Aw, maybe I should take you home, Josie."

"No, don't do that. We're already here. I can just wait in the car. It'll be fine."

"I'll stay with her," Fox said. "We'll lock the doors. It's a well-lit parking lot, and there are people everywhere. And we have our cell phones."

Mitch frowned. "I guess it'll be all right, if you think your aunt and uncle wouldn't mind. I'll try to hurry. Give me twenty minutes and then we'll get you home."

"Take your time," I said.

As soon as he was out of sight we grabbed our

backpacks and pulled on dark track pants and jackets over our clothes.

The marquee outside the Field House announced that there was a Frank Sinatra tribute concert that night. That explained the hundreds of cars in the parking lot.

We found a quiet corner outside the closed ticket office to talk strategy.

Fox checked his phone. "It's eight twenty. We have less than twenty minutes to get this done. It will be tougher than we thought with all these people around. Are you sure you can do this, Josie?"

A headache had started up behind my right eye, a persistent throb that set my already frazzled nerves on edge. I tried not to let it show. "Yes."

"It's just that you're not the best at being . . . sneaky."

"I'll be fine."

"Stick to places that are poorly lit."

My eye twitched. *I know.*

We split up to cover more ground, after Fox explained three more times how to be stealthy and not get caught. I had to shoo him away before I slapped him.

I felt a little foolish and a lot out of place among the clusters of college kids. They looked so cool and sophisticated and *tall*. I threw my shoulders back to gain an inch or two.

After a few minutes of searching, I spotted a narrow,

unlit passage and ducked in. A quick check with my flashlight confirmed that the alley was open at both ends. Good. An instant escape route.

Before I could talk myself out of it, I grabbed a can of spray paint, gave it a good shake, checked over both shoulders for witnesses, then quickly spelled out *BE-WARE* on the nearest wall.

I crouched down and stilled my breathing, waiting for the sound of approaching voices or footsteps. I wiggled my toes in my shoes to keep my feet from falling asleep, then realized I was wearing hard-soled sneakers. The sound of them slapping on the pavement as I made my escape wouldn't fool anyone. I took off the shoes, tied the laces together, and hung them around my neck. Saving hundreds of people was worth one ruined pair of socks.

Minutes later, I heard female voices coming closer. I slipped the goggles on, thumbed the power switch, and listened for the screams. The voices swelled—then passed right by and faded away.

Strike one.

I shuffled closer to the opening, ears straining for any telltale footsteps, when I heard a gasp and a whispered, "What's that? Caleb, do you see that?"

"Those red lights?" said a male voice. "It's probably an alarm system or something. Come on."

But the girl still stood, staring into the alley, backlit by a streetlight farther down the walkway, her expression fearful and curious. "Look," she whispered. "It's staring at us."

I held painfully still, wondering how long they would stand there.

"Kim." He tried to grab her arm. Now to add the finishing touch. I screwed my eyes shut and hissed at them.

Kim let out a startled shriek and took off running. "Kim!" Her friend jogged after her. I did a rousing victory dance in my head, careful to stay still on the outside. A minute passed, then two. Suddenly a commotion started up some distance away, shouts and running and a couple of screams.

Fox had been busy, no doubt, doing his job well as usual.

"Hey!"

The voice came from the alley entrance, just feet away. I jumped.

"I see it!"

My stomach jolted as I realized *I* was *it*.

"Get it!"

I ran. Footsteps thundered behind me. My shoes bounced against my collarbones. My jacket billowed out behind me, hopefully concealing the fact that I was shaped like a twelve-year-old girl and not like a towering half man, half moth. Nobody was supposed to actually chase me. My luck had held so far, but I knew as soon as the light from the other end of the alley hit me, I'd be discovered.

Better that than be caught outright, though. I dug deep for one more burst of speed, but stepped on a rock and felt my foot slide sideways and give out beneath me. I pitched forward, landing flat on my face, just as my pursuers closed the distance—

—and ran right past me.

I scrambled to hands and knees and crawled back the way I'd come. Shouts of "Where'd it go? It disappeared!"

drifted toward me. I froze, but the voices kept getting farther away.

I took off the goggles. Had it been enough? Should I find a new spot and try again? As I crouched there, indecisive, the moth pin pulsed with an unbearable burst of cold that doubled me over. I cried out, felt myself falling, the gravel and mud of the alleyway digging into my palms. A haze of red light filled my vision, and then I was back in the grassy field with Edgar, William, and Elsie . . .

* * *

"Quickly, now, Elsie. I'm getting bored."

"I—I choose . . ." She met William's eyes, then looked away. "I choose him. Kill him."

William's eyes filled. "Elsie . . ."

She would not look at William, so he turned to face Edgar, unflinching. "Yes. It should be me. Please, allow her to live, Edgar. Fear compels her. There is unselfishness in her heart. I know there is."

"We will see," Edgar said, and pulled the trigger.

He stepped over William's body to the sobbing Elsie. He pulled a gold pin from his pocket and affixed it to her collar.

She shrank from him, but he grabbed her arm in a cruel grip. "William believed you had kindness in you, but I see you for what you truly are. A bug to be collected and examined. Without affection, unworthy of mercy. Nothing more. Care to prove me wrong?

"This pin carries a curse of my own making. In the near future, I have foreseen that a terrible disaster will strike this town. You will be given a chance to prevent it." His eyes began to glow. "Save *every* victim and the curse is broken, but you will die. Your life for theirs.

"Do nothing and you live, but the victims will die. Their blood will be on your hands, and the curse will continue. *You* must decide who inherits the curse, or I will choose for you. Then the cycle will start again— another town, another disaster. I will provide a date and location. Nothing more.

"Perhaps you will try to stop the disaster and fail. You may die in the attempt, or live a long life of regret in the years to come. Either way, every unlucky fool who carries the curse will be trapped between worlds once they die, their souls doomed to torment. And know this: I will be working against you at every turn, spreading fear, thirsty for souls to join me in my misery. The misery you chose for me when you rejected me, then forced William to die in your place."

His eyes flared crimson. His shoulders hunched; wings sprouted. Elsie screamed . . .

. . . and so did I, a ragged gasp that tore from my raw, aching throat.

I awoke facedown, lying in a shallow puddle, the taste of gravel on my tongue. My muscles quivered and spasmed.

I rolled over and sat up, trying to make sense of what I'd just seen. To wrap my head around the fact that if I stopped the disaster, the curse had already sentenced me to death.

* * *

I drew my legs up and sat hugging my knees. My clothes were soaked through with muddy water, but I couldn't even feel it. The pin pulsed cold in perfect rhythm, a steady source of pain to match my stabbing headache. After a while, it occurred to me to take it off. The gold gleamed unnaturally bright in my palm, like a living thing.

A hand on my elbow made me jump.

But it was just Fox, trying to help me up. "We have to go," he said.

I couldn't get my arms or legs to work.

Fox grabbed my goggles and stuffed them into his bag. He put my shoes on for me and tied them like I was two years old.

"Josie?" He pulled at my arm. I stood and stumbled after him. He kept glancing at my face; I thought he could tell something was really wrong, but from the way he was hurrying, I guessed we didn't have time to stop and chat.

Students were gathered in groups here and there, their words high-pitched and hurried, buzzing about Mothman sightings. No one noticed us.

We made it back to Mitch's car just as the lights of a university police cruiser flashed, a second cruiser right behind, headed for the Field House.

I slipped out of my wet jacket and into the car. Fox climbed into the backseat beside me. Two minutes later, Mitch returned, his face looking pinched in the glow of the streetlights.

"What's going on?" Fox asked with just the right amount of worry in his voice as Mitch slid behind the wheel. "What's with all the cops?"

"I'm not sure," Mitch said. Larger groups of students were starting to gather, drawn to the red-and-blue lights like—well, like moths to a flame. Mitch rolled down the window and called to a nearby student. "Hey. Any idea what's happening?"

I waited, only half listening. Fox held his breath beside me.

"It's a Mothman sighting. This is so unreal. I have to call my roommate!"

Mitch rolled up the window. "More of this Mothman business. How can all these people be so gullible?" He glanced at us in the rearview mirror and gasped.

"Josie, you look awful. Are you all right? I shouldn't have left you."

I knew I was supposed to answer, but I couldn't stop shivering.

"It's been a long day," Fox said. "She'll feel better once we're home. Right, Josie?"

I managed to nod.

Mitch continued to watch us. Fox zipped up my backpack and placed it on the floor of the car. I was pretty sure a can of spray paint had been sticking out of it. Finally, Mitch put the car in drive and headed for home.

On the way, Fox showed me a few pictures he'd taken with his cell phone to document his handiwork. The messages were scrawled in ragged letters, with phrases like:

Many will perish

Remember Point Pleasant . . . Remember Clark . . . Athens is next . . .

And on the side of the Field House, impossibly huge:

Stay Out Monday

Danger

Death

"Extension pole," he whispered.

I blinked and nodded.

Aunt Barb had waited up for us, keeping half an eye on the die-hard Mothman followers still camped outside. After Mitch explained about my sudden illness, she fussed and felt my head and offered to make me some peppermint tea. I managed to convince her I was just exhausted and stumbled upstairs to my room.

Fox followed as soon as the coast was clear. "Aunt Barb's gone to bed," he said. Barb had been sleeping in Dad's room since Dad got hurt, just so she'd be close by. I was grateful she'd already turned in for the night.

"Josie, what happened? What's going on?"

I started to cry—the ugly, blubbery kind of crying with a runny nose and hiccups and shoulder-shaking sobs.

"Josie?"

"I don't want to die, Fox," I whispered.

"What?"

"The pin—when you took the pin off me in the Cave, the vision about Edgar, it must have ended early. To-night, in the alley"—I hiccuped—"I saw the rest of it. There really is a curse. If we stop the disaster, I'm gonna die. If we don't, I have to choose the next person to be cursed, and it starts all over again. I knew it. I knew it, deep down, Fox, as soon as I put on the pin. Maybe even before."

Horror and denial crossed Fox's face before he buried it deep and coaxed the whole story out of me.

"Bottom line," I said, staring at the pin with glassy eyes, "I can either save myself or a bunch of strangers. Some choice, huh?"

He shook his head. "No. I don't accept those choices. Maybe you misunderstood the vision. There must be a way to break the curse completely so that everyone makes it out alive."

I sniffed. "I don't think so. It's been a hundred years or more, and no one's managed to do it."

"You act like you've already given up. Well, *I'm* not giving up, so don't ask me to. You hear me? We'll figure this out."

"What, me and you? With Dad in the hospital and Aunt Barb stressed out of her mind and a mob of crazed Mothman groupies outside our door? I wish I could believe you. I'm going to die, and there's no way around it." I brushed at a spot of drying mud on my sleeve and heaved a shuddering sigh. "At least things couldn't possibly get any worse."

That's when we looked over and saw Mason standing in the doorway.

MASON'S LOWER LIP QUIVERED. HIS EYES were huge and round. I fumbled for anything I could possibly say to calm him down, but Fox was quicker. He slapped a hand over Mason's mouth, hustled him into the room, and shut the door. I wondered how much he'd heard.

"Josie, are you really gonna die?" Mason said. Fat tears rolled down his cheeks.

My heart broke into a thousand tiny pieces, sharp little shards that pierced me clean through. "No, honey. No." I knelt in front of him. "We just have to figure out how to stop something bad from happening, and then everything will be okay."

"Don't lie to him, Josie. He already heard us talking."

"He's too young for all this!"

"So are we! But it doesn't matter, does it? He already knows."

We both looked at Mason, who sniffled and wiped his nose on his sleeve. "Maybe I can help," he said.

I threaded my fingers through my messy hair. I didn't want him involved, but Fox was right. It was too late to take it back.

"Talk us through it, Josie," Fox prompted. "Tell us exactly what you saw, what you heard."

I sat on the floor across from them. I had their full attention.

"First of all, Mothman isn't causing the disasters. He sees them ahead of time. He provides a date and a place so the cursed person can try to save the victims, but he wants them to fail. He gives them this horrible choice just to make their lives miserable. It's all a big game to prove how selfish people are. It's sick."

"You're not selfish, Josie," Mason said.

"Thanks, Mason," I said, wishing I believed him. I explained everything I'd seen, everything I knew, while drawing patterns in the carpet without really seeing them. "So if I don't do anything to stop the disaster, I live, but all those people are doomed to die."

"And the curse continues," Fox said.

"Yes. And I have to choose who gets the pin next, or Mothman chooses for me."

"Option two?"

I swallowed. "If I stop the disaster, I break the curse, but I die."

Mason whimpered but otherwise kept silent.

"What if someone else stops it?" Fox said. "Like me."

"I don't know. I think no matter who stops it, I'm the one who has to die."

"What if we try to stop it and fail? All those people die, and the curse keeps going, but you live, right?" Fox said.

"Sure, but I still have to pick someone to be cursed. Either somebody I know, which I could never do, or a total stranger, which seems even worse." I decided not to mention the part about souls doomed to eternal torment. It was too awful to even think about.

"Does that mean Goodrich picked *you* to be cursed?"

"I think he was going to pick Dad," I said, voicing a suspicion that had been nagging at me. "Dad said John asked to meet with him, remember? Maybe after he talked to Dad, he couldn't go through with it. John killed himself two days later, and the pin was still in the safe. If he died without choosing someone, then it was up to Mothman."

"And you were the lucky winner," Fox said glumly.

Mason lifted my hand—the one still clutching the moth pin—and straightened my fingers one by one until he could see the pin where it lay on my palm, ugly and ominous. He stared at it, forehead creased in concentration. "Is this how you see the ghost?"

"Yes. His name is John."

"Maybe we could ask him what to do."

"He tries to help, but we can't hear him speak," I said.

His eyes lit up and he ran from the room.

Fox and I exchanged glances. I let my eyes fall closed, struggling to focus on anything other than the fear creeping in from all sides.

"So we need a plan," Fox said. "Two plans, actually. One to save those people, the other to make sure you survive."

Mason burst back into the room. "Maybe this will help!"

I opened my eyes to see him clutching the contraption he'd made from John's clock radio. "What is it, kiddo?"

"I heard the ghost's voice on my Batman radio. Maybe you could use this radio to talk to him again."

"Oh. That's . . . great. Good thinking, Mason. Thank you."

"Is he here now?" Mason said.

I looked down at the pin. With stiff, reluctant hands, I threaded the sharp end of the pin through my sleeve and looked around. "I don't see him."

"Maybe he'll talk to us anyway," Mason said.

We made a show of waiting, but the contraption sat silent and useless. Its days as a radio or anything else were over.

Mason's lower lip started up again.

"It's okay, Mason," I said. "It's so great that you tried."

"No! I have to help."

"You will. Maybe John's just not here right now."

Mason gave the device a good, solid kick before gathering it up in his arms. "I'll fix it," he said before marching off to his bedroom.

He should have been asleep in bed, but I didn't have the heart to shoot him down. He just wanted to help.

I heaved a weary sigh. I felt hollow. Empty. Devastated not just for myself, but for my brothers, too. "Do you think our vandalism made the news yet?"

A spark flashed in Fox's eyes, but it disappeared just as quickly. "If it worked—if our messages stopped the disaster, would you suddenly, you know—"

"Drop dead? I have no idea."

"I didn't mean it like that," Fox said, looking defeated. "I just think we should stop trying to prevent the disaster until we have a better idea of how to save you."

"But we already tried tonight, and I'm still here."

"Does that mean we failed?" he said.

"I don't really know how it works, but maybe this means I get until Monday before . . . you know. At least that would give us a fighting chance."

He stared at his hands, where streaks of red spray paint stained his skin. "I haven't talked to Dad all day," he whispered. "We don't even know how he's doing. He deserves to know about this, Josie."

I swallowed to soothe the painful knot in my throat. "What are we supposed to say? Where would we even start? It will kill him." I couldn't hold back the tears any longer. "I need—I need a few minutes, Fox. I just need to think for a minute. You could text Dad, see if he's still awake and ask how he's doing. Maybe check the news?"

I could see the muscles in his face twitch as he struggled with his own emotions. "Okay."

"Thank you."

When he left, I picked up the photo of Momma from my nightstand and hugged it to my chest. *What do I do, Momma?* I thought.

I remembered her in those last few days, thinner, skin pale and dull, eyes so tired, but still quick to laugh, still that smile filled with hope and love.

I'd asked her, *Are you scared?*

A little, she'd said. *But how we act when we're scared shows what kind of people we really are. Sometimes fear makes us want to run and hide, or get angry or sad. But it can also inspire us to do amazing things.*

Like what?

She lifted a hand to tuck a strand of hair behind my ear, but stopped short, lips quirking at my ragged haircut. *That's the best part. It's usually a surprise, even to us. A brave, beautiful surprise.*

* * *

Suddenly wide awake, I peeked in to find Mason asleep at the wrong end of his bed. I drifted downstairs. It was after ten o'clock. Fox had fallen asleep on the couch, remote control in hand. I switched off the TV, deciding I wasn't ready to hear how our little stunt had turned out just yet.

I shut myself in Dad's study, wanting to know what Elsie had decided. She was the first person Edgar had cursed. The *reason* for the curse. Obviously she hadn't ended it. But did she try?

I remembered the train derailment I'd read about in Ravenswood. There was also a note about it in one of John's journals. I pulled up the details online to refresh my memory. The Ohio River Railroad had just reached the town in 1886. Later that fall, a train jumped the track, killing thirty-one people, passengers and townspeople alike.

Next I found Elsie's obituary. It showed that she married Jacob Jeffreys in 1882 and moved to Missouri, where she had two children, seven grandchildren, and eventually died in Kansas City at age seventy. She was widowed in 1897 and never remarried.

So she didn't die in the disaster. And if she'd moved three states away, it didn't seem likely that she would have ever gone back just to warn a bunch of people who probably wouldn't have believed her anyway.

I rubbed at my eyes and shook my head.

Looked like Edgar was right about her. But if her soul was trapped with John and Nora and all the others, it seemed like an awfully harsh price to pay for a few bad choices, no matter how selfish.

I glanced at her husband's name again: Jacob Jeffreys. And he'd died in 1897. The name sounded familiar. After some more searching, I learned he was killed in a factory fire in Ohio. What were the chances he would die in a major disaster in Ohio, after he and Elsie had moved away fifteen years before? Could it be? Was he the next to be cursed?

Then it clicked. In that 1902 interview I'd found, the politician had said he'd received a way to predict tragedy from longtime friend Jacob Jeffreys.

A clearer picture of the pin's journey started to form. I grabbed John's journals and the notes he'd already made. The information was incomplete, but he hadn't had the Internet to help him.

Maybe knowing the path the pin had taken through the years wouldn't help me figure out how to save a building full of people, but it might reveal some over-looked detail that could put an end to the curse once and for all.

* * *

The next morning, I stumbled downstairs after managing about three hours of sleep. I could hear Aunt Barb doing dishes in the kitchen and muttering to herself. I peeked out the front window. A few clusters of die-hard Mothman fans were still camped in the cow pasture, though most had the good sense to go home.

Fox and Mason were already awake, faces grim, eyes glued to the TV. When they saw me, they scooted to either side to make room on the couch.

"I'm sorry I fell asleep last night," Fox whispered. "How are you holding up?"

I shrugged, not feeling up for conversation just yet. My marathon research session had been a bust.

A woman's tear-streaked face filled the screen. She was looking off to one side, lost in memory. "My grandmother lived in Point Pleasant when Mothman came. She saw him, about a month before the bridge fell. She told me those red eyes would haunt her for the rest of her life."

An interviewer offscreen prompted, "And I understand you were at the auction yesterday?"

"Yes. I saw him. I saw his red eyes. They were real.

Something terrible is going to happen in Athens." She dabbed at her face with a tissue. "What can any of us do to stop it?"

That sounded promising. I looked at Fox hopefully, but he shook his head and changed the channel.

Local reporter Molly Madigan stood in front of the Field House clutching her microphone.

"If you're just joining us, we're at Ohio University, where there were multiple sightings of the moth creature last night, as well as several acts of vandalism." The screen cut to shaky footage of someone running. You couldn't see him, but you could hear his rough breathing and rapid footfalls. Suddenly the camera zoomed in on a pair of red eyes that hovered in a dark alley for several seconds, then disappeared. I knew it was just Fox or me in a pair of Halloween goggles, but it was still eerie as all get-out.

Molly reappeared on-screen. "Witnesses disagree on whether what they saw was real. But whatever the case, a new trend has exploded overnight." The scene changed to crowds of students mugging for the camera, every last one of them wearing red-eye goggles.

The camera panned to some enterprising college kid sitting behind a fold-up table, selling the goggles for twenty dollars a pair. His name flashed on-screen: *Stuart Jenkins: Business Major, Entrepreneur.*

Molly approached Stuart with her trusty microphone. "Tell me, Stuart, is this all in good fun, or are you capitalizing on people's fears?"

"Oh, all in good fun, Molly."

"And how did you acquire your merchandise so quickly?"

"A late-night run to the Home Depot and some good, old-fashioned elbow grease," he said with a wink. "I would like to reassure our valued customers that I have recently hired a production team to assist me in assembling sufficient inventory." Another guy stepped into the shot, waving and mouthing, "Hi, Mom!"

Molly pressed on, unfazed. "Some of the messages said to stay away from the Field House tomorrow, didn't they? Do your actions at all diminish those who are genuinely afraid of what the reemergence of Mothman might mean for Athens?"

"Not at all. I feel that humor is a valuable tool in helping us deal with those fears. Besides, rumor has it a certain rival basketball team is behind these so-called warnings. But it won't keep fans of our local Athens High Bulldogs from supporting their team tomorrow night. I urge every true Bulldog fan to purchase a pair of these goggles to prove we will not be intimidated."

"What would you say to those who would suggest

that last's night's sightings were all a stunt to promote sales of your new business?"

"Absolutely false."

"Are you worried about competition?"

"A little healthy competition never hurt anyone." He slipped a pair of the goggles over his face and switched them on. "I'm more than happy to share the wealth."

"And there you have it. Whether an honest multiple sighting or a brilliant marketing campaign, a new trend has definitely arrived here on campus. Ron, back to you."

By that time, the three of us were slumped so low in our seats we could barely see the TV.

Uncle Bill came in from outside and dropped the morning's paper on the table. The giant headline read, MULTIPLE MOTH SIGHTINGS AT OU START NEW FASHION TREND; COPYCATS SURE TO FOLLOW.

"That moth gets around," he said between sips of his morning coffee, which he drank standing up before sauntering out toward the auction building to prep for the Goodrich auction do-over.

"Okay, so chances are we haven't stopped anything," Fox said. "But maybe that's not such a bad thing. It gives us time to regroup, figure this out."

I nodded, grateful he was staying positive. But we were desperately short on time and ideas.

"Hey, by the way, we're going to see Dad this morning. Aunt Barb said she'd take us."

"We are?" I was equal parts thrilled and horrified. What would I say to him?

"Listen, I talked to him for a minute this morning," Fox said.

"Does he know about the Mothman sightings?"

"Yes. Uncle Bill told him. He's pretty frantic about it all. He asked me if I saw it, if I thought it was real."

"What did you say?"

"I said yes."

"And?" I prompted. "What did he say?"

"Pretty much what we already guessed," Fox said. "That he saw Mothman at the Goodrich house, but he didn't think anyone would believe him."

"Did you say anything about the curse?"

Fox sent an uneasy glance toward the kitchen. "No. I thought I should talk to you first."

Relief washed through me. If we told Dad, I wanted to be the one to do it.

"Josie, there's something else. They might let him come home tomorrow."

"But tomorrow's Monday." I felt sick knowing he might come home on the very day everything imploded. I should have been looking forward to having him back. Instead, all I could think about was how to get past him if he tried to stop me from going to the Field House.

When we got to the hospital, Dad looked almost like his old self. We all gave him huge hugs, and he hugged us extra tight right back. For Mason's sake, we kept talk of Mothman to a minimum. Then I asked if I could have a minute with Dad to myself. But as soon as we were alone, he told me how worried he'd been, how frustrating it was to be stuck in the hospital, and how glad he was to see us all safe.

So much for telling him about the curse. I couldn't do it. I managed to keep the tears from falling until I hugged him goodbye and left the room. Luckily Fox was the only one who noticed.

* * *

By the time we got home, I was barely keeping the panic at bay. "Fox, maybe we should divide and conquer," I told him. "I can work on finding out more about the curse and ways to break it. And I need you and Mason to brainstorm every possible way to keep people out of the Field House tomorrow."

"We're on it." He ducked his head to look me in the eye. "How are you, really?"

"I'm functioning. That'll have to be enough for now."

"Hey!"

Aunt Barb's voice from the kitchen nearly made me jump out of my skin.

"You people need to get a life. This is a private residence!"

Fox and I peeked into the kitchen. Aunt Barb was leaning out an open window, scolding a group of Mothman fans who'd gotten too close to the house.

"Those are flower beds, you ninny!" she shouted.

"You okay, Aunt Barb?" I asked from a safe distance.

She whirled on us, her face a mask of righteous fury. She pasted on a smile and smoothed the wrinkles from her shirt. "Everything is right as rain. I just have a little dispute to settle."

She marched outside with a rolling pin in her hand. We heard her launch into a sermon about perennials and people with less sense than God gave a speck of dirt.

"Guess she's had her fill of Mothman," Fox said.

"Me too."

* * *

I headed back to Dad's office to try again. I sat at the desk, comforted by the reminders of Dad all around me: an antique wooden gavel, a bag of sunflower seeds, and a coffee mug we'd given him for Christmas that said, AUCTIONEER BY DAY, NINJA BY NIGHT.

I lapsed into a daze of morbid thoughts. *Would I ever*

get to drive a car? Kiss a boy? See the world? I took apart the curse in my head, piece by piece, weighing my impossible options:

1. Be a horrible, selfish human being and let a lot of people die, then pass the curse on to someone else.
2. Try to stop the disaster, fail, and live with the guilt for the rest of my life. And still pass the curse on to someone else.
3. Die a hero but leave my family to grieve for another loved one.

I let myself imagine doing nothing, allowing others to be killed so I could keep breathing. *What if only ten people were in danger? Five? What if only one person was doomed to die in the disaster—someone who'd already lived a long, happy life? Could I ignore it then?*

Yes, I thought stubbornly, because I was young and had dreams, and because my family had already lost Momma.

No, I thought with my next breath. If I could save even one person—someone with their own dreams and family—then I had to try. I felt sick that I could even think about acting as Elsie had. So much for option one.

I skipped over option two, since I couldn't bear to imagine letting all those people down.

Option three, then. Would it hurt to die? Maybe if it was just for a few seconds it wouldn't be so bad. Especially if I ended up saving lives. Maybe people would put up a statue of me, or start a scholarship in my name.

I cringed. Somehow it always came back to my own selfish wants.

Maybe that was Edgar's whole point.

So many questions nagged at me: Could Dad handle another loss? Would I become a ghost like John Goodrich? And the one question that had sunk its teeth into me and wouldn't let go:

Would I see Momma again?

ALL THE WORRYING WAS WASTING PRECIOUS time. I forced myself to focus. I was about to reach for one of John's journals when a book from the storeroom caught my eye, called *The Lingering Spirit*. When I picked it up, it fell open to a dog-eared page with a chapter heading that read: *Suicides, Violent Deaths, and Other Earthly Traumas.*

I skimmed a highlighted passage: *Certain types of deaths are prone to creating spirits that linger on earth rather than passing to the other side. Crime victims, suicides, and those with a strong sense of unfinished business are the most commonly encountered class of ghostly manifestations. Eyewitness accounts confirm that these spirits are more likely to exhibit characteristics of the living, such as speech, a realistic human form, and the ability to manipulate solid objects.*

I read it again. Suddenly it all made sense. John was dying, so he had ended his life early as a last-ditch effort to stay in the game, to offer his help. How *much* help he'd actually provided seemed iffy at best, but at least his heart was in the right place.

Sighing, I stared at something odd on a corner of the desk. I realized it was the remains of Mason's contraption, piled in a messy heap. I couldn't help a fond chuckle. It hadn't been such a bad idea, really. We did hear John's voice over the radios in the storeroom . . .

I sat up straighter. Could it really be that simple?

I glanced around the office and spotted a 1940s Bakelite radio on one of the shelves. It was one of Dad's favorite finds. But did it still work?

I took it down and plugged it in. I held my breath and switched it on.

Nothing . . . wait. The dials were lit up. Maybe it just wasn't tuned to any station. I turned up the volume and heard the hiss of static. I twisted the dial slowly, slowly, pausing each time I heard a voice, until—

"Josie."

My head jerked up. John stood on the other side of the desk. I realized I was still wearing my sweatshirt from the night before, the pin jabbed through the sleeve.

"John?"

"Save them." The voice was faint, wrapped in static, and layered as if several people were speaking together but couldn't quite get the timing right.

I stood slowly. "John, I can hear you! The radio!"

He looked as surprised as I felt. "Save them," he said.

"Yes! Yes, save them! I hear you. Wait, I have to get Fox. Don't go anywhere!"

I found the boys in Fox's room and dragged them downstairs to the study. Once behind closed doors again, I declared, "John, say it again. Go ahead."

"Save them."

"You heard that, right?" I said.

"Yeah," Fox said.

"Wow," Mason said.

They both stared at the radio, spellbound. "You had the right idea, Mason," Fox said.

Mason grinned.

"Save them."

I huffed a frustrated breath. "Can't you say anything else? I just found out that the curse comes with a death sentence. I need answers, John. You killed yourself hoping your ghost could help us, right? Then *help us*."

"Wait, really?" Fox said.

"Father. Your father," John said. "Chose him to end it. There was a letter. In the safe. There was a letter."

"We didn't find any letter, John," Fox said. "Just a little scrap of paper with your favorite phrase on it."

"Save them."

"Yep. That's what it said."

"It's like he's stuck," I said. "Like his thoughts are getting scrambled between here and . . . wherever he is."

"Save them. Save you. I died," John said. "Died early. Early . . . to *save them. Save you.*"

"I thought you did it because you were too sick to stop the disaster," I said.

"More. There's more," John said. "I already died. Now save them."

I closed my eyes, trying to fill in the missing pieces. "What if his death has already satisfied the curse?" I

217

said. "So if we manage to stop the disaster, then I won't die and it all ends. That makes sense, right?"

I looked over at the boys for their reaction. Mason shrugged, but Fox looked thoughtful.

"Please tell us, John," Fox said. "If we save them, does it mean Josie won't die after all?"

John looked at each of us in turn, eyes pleading. "Save them. Save you."

"He doesn't know," I said, disappointment turning my words brittle.

"But it makes sense. That's good enough for me," Fox said, his jaw set. He turned to leave.

"Where are you going?" I asked.

"Out."

He swung the door wide and headed for the front entryway. Mason looked at me in alarm. "Josie?"

"Go and stall him," I said. "I'll be right there."

"Edgar is angry," John said.

That made me pause. "You and Mothman are on a first-name basis? That's new."

John bared his teeth; his eyes narrowed in sudden fury. Cold air crept along the floor from every corner and circled my feet. "Hate him. I hate him."

I took a step back, unnerved by his change of mood. "I don't blame you, John. But I need to know. Do you know *for sure* that I won't die if we save those people?" He blinked at me, his anger fading, and shook his head.

"That's just great."

His image began to flicker.

"No, don't go. Please, John, I need you, because I think Fox is about to do something really stupid!"

"Save them," John whispered, and disappeared.

"*Arrrrrggghhh!*" I kicked the desk before hurrying out of the study with a brisk limp. "Fox, where do you think you're going?"

"No more screwing around. We stop the disaster, you live. And I know a foolproof way, right now, to make sure there are no people in that building tomorrow."

"What are you gonna do?"

"Nothing." He wouldn't meet my eye. "I'll see you later."

Mason clung to Fox's arm. He looked fearfully from me to Fox and back again.

"Fox."

"The less you know, the better, Josie."

"It doesn't work that way! We're in this together."

"Not this time. I know you hate breaking the rules, but one of us has to, so better if it's me."

"You really think you're gonna burn the Field House to the ground?" I snapped.

Mason's eyes got round and huge.

I herded them both into the kitchen. "The building is practically new. It's probably got all kinds of fancy systems to protect it."

"All I have to do is damage it enough to cancel Monday's events. It's the only way to know for sure that we've stopped it."

"No, it isn't. Say you manage to burn up some crucial support structure. What if people are in there tomorrow, looking for the cause of the fire, and the roof collapses?"

He huffed. "I'll figure something out. I'm not gonna let my sister die because of some stupid curse. Just let me end it!"

"No. I can't let you do this. John killed himself on a hunch—do you get that? He did something stupid out of desperation. Just like you're about to do. What if I drop dead the minute you set fire to the building?"

His forehead scrunched in confusion. "But . . . Goodrich said . . ."

"The truth is, we don't know what will happen."

He shook his head. "And you think that's going to change before tomorrow?"

"I'm saying we still have time to figure this out."

"And if I disagree, then you're gonna stop me? What are you gonna do, tell on me?"

"Oh, I'll stop you," I said, balling up my fists "Mason, you'd better move, honey."

Mason backed away.

"This ought to be good," Fox said. "She'll stop me, she says. Like she has any chance of—*ack!*"

I ducked my head, led with one shoulder, and charged. My tackle hit him center mass, right in the chest. He took me down with him, along with a couple of kitchen chairs, as he was knocked off his feet. He landed on his butt with a satisfying "*Oof!*"

I pinned him in a wrestling hold I'd seen him use on Mason multiple times. "Give up?"

He bucked, quicker than I'd thought possible, tossing me to the side and rolling to his feet in one skillful move.

I grabbed the closest thing at hand—the broom—and leveled it at him. "You're not going anywhere, Fox."

He backed up toward the sink, grabbed the spray nozzle, and yanked the hose out as far as it would go.

"Don't you dare!" I shouted.

"Drop the broom," he said.

"No."

"What are you gonna do with a broom, anyway? Sweep me to death?" He squeezed the trigger, just for a second, but it was enough to drench me in cold water.

I shrieked and dropped the broom.

"Had enough?"

Hardly. I spotted a black Sharpie on the counter and went for that instead. I ripped the cap off and held the pen like a dagger, jabbing it in Fox's direction.

He flinched, just long enough for me to move in for a second strike and draw a long swipe of black across his forearm and onto his favorite shirt. He stared at the mark in horror, then lifted his eyes to mine, expression flashing from offended disbelief to steely anger. "Oh, it is *on*."

He squeezed the nozzle trigger and held it down. I shrieked again and tried to dance out of the stream of water, managing to put two black lines across the back of his hand. "You're not the only one who can fix this!" I shouted. "Good old Fox. He'll make it right, because he's so *perfect*!"

Fox reached out and slapped the pen from my grip. I seized the hose snaking out from the sink and bent it in half, cutting off his precious water supply.

"What is going on here?"

Aunt Barb stood in the doorway, hands on hips.

I let go of the hose, realizing too late Fox was pointing it right at Barb. She shouted as water drenched her. I reached over and turned off the faucet, but the damage was done.

Then Fox did something that I never thought I'd see: he ran. Didn't make up some outrageous story on the spot, didn't try to charm his way out of trouble. He just dropped the sprayer, ran upstairs to his room, and slammed the door.

The house felt like a kettle about to wail.

Mason huddled in the corner, crying.

Aunt Barb stood, sopping wet, breathing heavily, staring around the kitchen at the mess we'd made—chairs knocked over, boxes of cereal spilled across the floor in colorful constellations.

Someone pounded on the front door.

Aunt Barb leaned against a chair and heaved a mighty sigh. "What now?"

I grabbed a towel and handed it to her, then grabbed another for myself. "I'll get it. Mason?" I said on my way out of the kitchen. "I'm sorry we were fighting. Give me just a minute, okay?" I swung the door open to find two police officers on the porch. And Mitch, of all people, stood behind them, fidgeting.

"Um, Aunt Barb? The police are here."

She bustled into the living room, fussing with her wet hair. "Why, hello, officers," she said, voice dripping with honey. "How are you on this fine day? Would you care for some blueberry muffins?"

"We need to speak with your husband, Mrs. Reevey."

"Why, is that you, Jake? I haven't seen you since that summer you were mowing lawns to save for college."

Jake, the younger of the two cops, cleared his throat. "Yes, ma'am. Is Bill here?"

"He's out in the auction house, I'm sure. Mason, honey, run and fetch him, would you?"

Mason stared at the group on the porch for a good minute before edging past them and running across the yard.

"Well, come in, come in, have a seat." Aunt Barb bustled about in her housedress, looking like a big, wet poodle, still trying to make everyone feel at home. "Can I get you some coffee?"

Mitch and the policemen stepped inside but did not sit. "No, thank you, ma'am."

"Mitch," she said, "are you still enjoying your work here at Fletcher Auctions?"

He shuffled his feet, cleared his throat. "Uh, yes, ma'am."

"Is that so? Would you like to continue making chit-chat, then, or would you like to tell me the real reason you all are here?"

I heard Fox's bedroom door open upstairs, followed by careful footsteps in the hall.

Mitch kept his gaze on the ground. "I'm sorry, Mrs. Reevey. You've all been so good to me. But what your husband is doing is wrong. Making your niece and nephew play along is even worse. Trying to fool people like that . . ."

"Fool people—officers, what is this all about?"

Uncle Bill and Mason walked in.

Officer Jake stepped forward, one of our auction flyers clutched in his hand. "Bill Reevey, I'm afraid you're under arrest for destruction of public property, fraud, and child endangerment."

I sucked in a startled breath.

"No!" Fox shouted, pounding down the stairs. "He didn't do anything wrong."

"Hush up now," Uncle Bill said. "Can you at least tell me when and where I did all these things?"

"Sir, it would be better if we take you to the station to discuss things there. You have the right to remain silent . . ."

"No, you can't take him. It was me, all right?" Fox shouted. "Whatever you're accusing him of, it was all me, my idea, trying to drum up some business around here."

"And me," I jumped in. "Mitch will tell you. He drove us to the campus the other night. Please."

"These kids did nothing wrong, officers," Uncle Bill said. "I'm happy to go down to the station to straighten all this out."

Aunt Barb fanned her face with one hand. "I sincerely hope you are not accusing us of dreaming up this Mothman spectacle. Anyone with two eyes could see that creature was real."

Everyone started talking and shouting at once. Uncle Bill gave a piercing whistle that shut us all up quick. He motioned for Jake to join him on the porch. "May I speak to you outside, please?" he asked with his typical calm.

Fox turned to Mitch. "Mothman is real," he said. "And everyone who was at the auction knows it. Hundreds of people saw him!"

Mitch paled but shook his head in denial. "It was a trick, simple as that."

Mason hurried over to tug on my sleeve. "Josie, are they taking Uncle Bill to jail?"

I slipped an arm around him. "Yes." I didn't have the energy to dance around the truth anymore.

"I need to change into some dry clothes. Don't let them leave without me," Aunt Barb said, hurrying upstairs.

After a few minutes, Uncle Bill and Jake came back into the house. The older cop pulled out his handcuffs, but Uncle Bill said, "You don't need those." Jake shook his head and his partner put the cuffs away. Together they ushered Uncle Bill outside to the police cruiser.

Mitch followed them out and stood awkwardly on the porch, like he wanted to say something to us. I glared at him. "You don't know what you've done," I told him. "I don't care if you meant well or not. You may have just doomed hundreds of people to die."

"I just hope you and your family get the help you need, Josie," Mitch said, not meeting my gaze.

Fox stormed toward us, no doubt some silver-tongued insult on his lips, but I stepped in front of him just in time. "Goodbye, Mitch," I said, and softly closed the door.

"Why'd you do that? I still had plenty to say to him."

"He thinks he's helping," I said with a sigh.

Aunt Barb returned, dressed and mostly dry, her wild hair tamed into submission and pinned on top of her head. "What a mess," she said, shaking her head. "I have to go with them to straighten all this out. You three will be okay on your own, won't you? I could call some-one . . ."

"We'll be fine," I said quickly. "You just have to convince them that Uncle Bill didn't do anything wrong. Please."

"I've already called our lawyer. Don't worry." She folded each of us into a hug before lining us up shoulder-to-shoulder across the living room, her face stern. "You will mop up all this water while I'm gone, and clean up this mess." We nodded. "Whatever all this fighting is about, it stops now, understood?" We nodded again. "Warm up some leftovers for lunch. Keep the doors locked. Keep your cell phones charged. And try not to worry. In a few days, this will all seem like a bad dream."

We watched her go in silence. None of us could think of anything to say.

Mason switched on the TV and curled up on the couch with a blanket while Fox and I cleaned up the kitchen. I could hear a reporter talking about the annual Mothman Festival, a two-day party in Point Pleasant with vendors, music, and guest speakers.

His segment was interrupted by a sudden burst of "breaking news" theme music. Fox and I dropped our mops and ran for the living room.

A local reporter, his face solemn, appeared on-screen. "There has been a fresh wave of Mothman sightings this morning. Reports are coming in from all over Athens, along with dozens of amateur videos."

"Could it be a hoax?" Fox wondered, but then we saw the first video.

"This recording, submitted by Brad Sutter, was taken outside the Walmart on State Street. As you can see, several dozen eyewitnesses were on the scene."

Fox grabbed up the remote and stabbed the volume button with his thumb.

"That's really him," I said.

We watched Mothman hover over the parking lot, swooping, diving, sending people running for cover. The next video was shot in a neighborhood full of fancy brick houses, the next on a wooded road. They all showed pretty much the same thing.

"What is he up to?" Fox said.

"Why is he so mad, Josie?" Mason wondered.

"John said that, too."

"Said what?" Fox said.

"He said Edgar . . . Mothman . . . was angry."

Fox snorted. "Has he ever been anything else?"

We stared at the TV as the videos replayed again and again.

"Watch him," I said. "Do you notice anything weird?"

Fox shrugged. "I don't know. He's just flying around like he did at the auction. Why?"

"Exactly. It's the same in every single video. He

doesn't hurt anyone. He doesn't break anything. He just . . . watches. It has to mean something."

"I'm listening," Fox said.

"It's like, everybody has a weakness, right? As Mothman, he has certain powers, but maybe there are rules he has to follow, too. Or . . . or maybe there was something he had to give up."

"Like my comic books," Mason said. "There's always a way to beat the bad guy, even when he has super-strength or he's really smart."

I felt a tiny flicker of hope. "Exactly. Good thinking, Mason." I took off the pin and rubbed my thumb across the glass. "But if we're going to take Mothman down, we need to know more about that curse."

16

WE GATHERED UP EVERY LAST ITEM WE'D taken from the storeroom—books, journals, scrapbooks, photo albums, and papers—and huddled around the coffee table with the radio from Dad's office.

But I realized something was missing. Goodrich's moth shadow box had been on my mind, and I decided it might be time for another look. "Be right back," I said before running upstairs and pulling the shadow box from beneath a pile of too-small sweaters in the back of my closet.

When I returned to the living room, Mason was fiddling with the radio while Fox paged through the *Lingering Spirit* book.

"Did you know that animals can come back as spirits, too?" Fox said.

"Cool," Mason said.

"Is that helpful in some way?" I said.

"Nah. Just interesting."

I put on the pin, right up near the pulse point in my neck. "John?" I called. "Are you here?"

"Yes."

He stood near the kitchen, image flickering.

"Did this shadow box belong to Edgar?" I asked.

"Yes."

"How did you know, Josie?" Fox said. "And how did Goodrich get his hands on it?"

"It was just a hunch. He had forty years and a whole lot of money to track down some of Edgar's old things. Plus John doesn't really seem like the kind of guy who collected bugs. Right, John?"

The look of disgust on John's face backed me up. I turned the shadow box over. A board had been nailed into place as the backing; I would need something to pry it loose. I nabbed a pair of scissors from the kitchen and plopped down on the floor beside my brothers. Hope made my pulse pound and my fingers fumble, but at last I was able to slide a scissor blade beneath the wood and lift. The thin wood resisted, resisted, then splintered beneath the force. Tossing the scissors aside, I tore at the board with my bare hands. I could already see a second backing underneath and the telltale corner of a yellowed piece of paper. I grabbed up the scissors again and stabbed through the wood backing over and over, reducing it to kindling.

Mason watched the destruction, nodding his approval.

Finally I was able to slide my hand through the opening and pull the paper free, getting several splinters in the process. This had to be the answer we'd been looking for.

It had to be.

The paper had become brittle with age. With great care, I unfolded it and stared down at the spidery black handwriting there, slashing its way across the page in angry strokes.

It was the same hand that had scrawled *MINE MINE MINE* across the walls of the Cave.

Edgar.

I read hungrily, eagerly, eyes skipping across the words like stones on a pond.

Edgar had copied down the spell he'd used to seal the curse, but there was nothing about reversing or breaking it. When I reached the end, I read it again, then turned it over to make sure there was nothing written on the back. I handed the paper to Fox before grabbing up the shadow box and shaking it. No other pieces of paper fell out. I seized the nearest heavy object within reach—Dad's muddy old work boot—and used it to break the glass, obliterating the moths beneath. When I'd smashed the whole thing to bits, I pawed through the pile of rubble, but there was nothing else.

"Uh, I think it's toast, Josie," Fox said.

"That's it?" I knelt there amid the mess. What good did it do me to know that Edgar's spell called for graveyard dirt and raven's bones, eye of moth and an outlaw's ashes? "John, did you know this was in here?"

"Yes."

"Did it help you?"

A wry look replaced his usual sad expression. "No."

"I need to know more about this spell! How many

people want to turn themselves into a half man, half moth who can see future disasters? There's no way he just found this in a book somewhere. He must have had help. There must be more to it! Do you know, John? Did you ever find anything, see anything?"

"No. Edgar kept his secrets well," he said.

"If Mothman is the only one who knows, then we're finished," I said. Mason slid closer to me. Fox had his nose buried in the book. "Fox, are you hearing me?"

"Yeah. Just a second."

Eventually he looked up, marking his place with one finger. "Is it safe to say the pin is *linked* to Mothman? I mean, you've seen visions of his past through it, right?"

"You know I have."

"And John is still linked to the pin because the curse is still active, and that's how you're able to see him."

"That sounds about right."

He handed me the open book. "Have you ever heard of spirit walking?"

I scanned the page. "You mean like an out-of-body experience?"

"Yeah. I don't think it's that different from what you've already done."

I read a passage out loud: "'The living and the dead may walk together on the psychic plane when other attempts to communicate fall short. The process requires a magical object or conduit, preferably an object owned by the spirit in life. This creates a link that allows the living subject to see and experience what the spirit has seen.'"

"But John hasn't seen how the curse was created," I said.

"You're both still linked to Mothman, right?"

We nodded, girl and ghost, though no one could see John but me.

"And you happen to have a piece of paper from the exact event you want to relive. The book calls that an artifact. It can help guide your movements."

John looked hopeful, even excited.

"You haven't tried this before?" I asked him.

"No."

"Then what are we waiting for? What do we have to do?"

* * *

They sat me down on the couch and surrounded me with pillows. I caught Fox watching me, chewing his lip. "Are you sure about this, Josie?" he said. "How do we know it's safe?"

"We don't, but we're almost out of time."

Fox and Mason shared a worried glance.

"Please, I have to try. Tell me what to do."

Fox traced his finger down the page. "The person and the spirit are supposed to touch the conduit at the same time and focus on a destination."

"That's it?"

"I think so."

"Don't forget the spell." Mason handed it to me and I clutched it tight.

"Are you ready, John?"

He moved closer and reached out with one hand. I leaned away out of reflex. I felt the air grow cold at his approach. Our eyes met. I saw doubt and worry in his face as his icy fingers stretched toward my collar.

Fox leapt to his feet even though he couldn't see John. "Josie, I changed my mind, I don't think you should—"

But it was too late.

The moment John "touched" the pin, I was falling, sightless, flailing, so cold I thought I might shatter—

* * *

We were standing in John's house in Clark, at the top of the stairs. John still appeared in black and white, as if leached of all color. I looked down at myself to find that I was black and white, too.

"It worked! Am I a ghost?"

"No. Only your consciousness is with me here. What some people call the mind or the soul."

I smiled at the sound of his voice—his real voice. "I can understand you. You make a lot more sense now."

"Communicating as a ghost is not as easy as the book led me to believe. There are . . . obstacles. It is indeed a luxury to have a real conversation with you. It beats writing on walls."

Tilting my head, I studied his face. "Why do you look like you did forty years ago, instead of what you looked like when you died?"

He crossed his arms. "Do you mean old?"

"Well . . . yeah."

"This was my age when I first put on the pin. The day the landslide took my Nora."

I met his gaze. "I'm so sorry, John."

His lips thinned. He looked at his shoes. "It was a long time ago."

He pointed at an envelope that lay at the base of the wall, near his feet. "This is the letter that was meant for your father."

"I can't believe the answer was here all along and we missed it."

"Not precisely," John said. "I only explained the basics about stopping the disaster and gave strict instructions not to touch the pin, just to be safe. I didn't think it would be necessary to address the curse at all. I truly believed I could end it."

"By taking your own life?"

"Yes. My body was failing. I did not know if I would live until the day of the disaster. Your father is well respected in Athens. I thought people would listen to him. I never intended to curse him, only ask for his help, but as soon as I met him face-to-face I realized what I had to say would be perceived as the ravings of a damaged mind. I thought as a spirit I could not only convince him the danger was real, but also fulfill the sacrifice the curse required once the disaster was averted. I am sorry for what happened to your father, and even more sorry the curse has fallen to you."

He waved a hand and suddenly we were downstairs, staring out the picture window with a clear view of the ruined mountain.

"Edgar and I had nothing but time, Josie. He had no control over when the next disaster would happen. All we could do was wait. For forty years. There were other, smaller disasters in that time, but after Clark, Mothman got a taste for large-scale loss of life. He waited until something big was on the horizon—the Field House. From the day I was cursed to the day the Field House is under threat—it's the longest stretch of time since the curse began.

"He visited me more and more as the years went by, wanting to pass the time, to educate me about how misunderstood he was. I think by the end he considered us friends. But I hated him—for taking Nora from me, for creating the curse in the first place."

"How did you communicate? Mothman can't speak, can he?"

"Through the pin. When I wore it, I could hear him in my head, feel what he was feeling. Only rarely at first, but more and more as the years passed. Edgar came and went at his leisure. He showed me glimpses of his life growing up. Other disasters he's witnessed. But I never saw the birth of the curse itself. He kept it from me, guarded it closely. But hopefully that is about to change. Are you ready?"

I nodded. I concentrated as hard as I could on the spell.

Flickers of light and shadow filled my vision and I felt myself falling as John took my hand and said, "Hold on tight."

* * *

Edgar sat across from an old hag, her body bent with age. Her shriveled hands were folded on the table, her face creased and scarred.

"You wish me to fashion a spell for you?"

"I want revenge." He set the moth pin on the table and pushed it toward her. "And I want this to be the source." I could *feel* Edgar's desperation, his anger and madness.

"Yes, this will do nicely," she said, examining the pin, her black eyes shining.

"So you can do it?"

The hag fixed her gaze on him. "You wish to destroy yourself and countless others over a woman? Are you certain she is worth it?"

He slammed his hand on the table. "She is worth nothing. But hurting her and others like her is worth everything to me."

"What manner of skills do you seek?"

"Foresight. I wish to know when and where disaster will strike."

"Is that all?"

"I desire a frightening form. An insect, something that will cause people to recoil in fear."

"Anything else?"

"I want to live forever."

Her eyes flashed. "You ask a great deal of me."

"Is it beyond your skill?"

"Hardly." The hag stood, choosing books from a shelf behind her and tossing them on the table. She spent several minutes paging through each one and choosing jars and glass vessels from around the room that were filled with exotic-looking plants and herbs, powders and potions.

She set a small iron cauldron in the center of the table and began adding ingredients.

"I grant you the form of half man, half moth. Grotesque and fearsome, you will strike terror in the hearts of all who look upon you. The cost is your humanity, your connection with the outside world. Touch anyone or anything, and the curse is broken. You may only observe, never interfere."

"Agreed."

She opened the wide plank door and held a lantern out into the darkness. Insects swarmed to the flickering flame. She reached out and snatched a moth from the air, swung the door closed, and crumbled the moth in her hand before dropping it into the cauldron.

"I grant you the gift of foresight, but only as it pertains to future calamities within a hundred miles as the crow flies, north, south, east, and west of this very site. The cost is . . . your tongue. Agreed?"

He swallowed. "Yes."

"Whomever you curse with the pin must stop a disaster of your choosing. Every victim must be saved, or the curse continues."

The hag pushed a quill, a bottle of ink, and a piece of

coarse paper across the table toward him. "Write down the words I speak. It is the spell you will read to activate the curse, when you are ready. Be quick; I will not say it twice."

His eyes shone with vengeful glee as she named ingredients and whispered ominous-sounding phrases. His fingers twitched as he wrote, as if impatient to move things along. "What of my last request to become immortal?"

"Granted—so long as the curse goes unbroken."

"And the cost?"

She smiled, revealing several gold teeth. "Your soul."

Using a pair of tongs she lifted a crucible of molten gold from an iron stove and tipped it until a single drop fell into the cauldron. After pounding and mixing the ingredients with a stone pestle, she threw the pin into the cauldron while muttering to herself. A burst of light, a puff of smoke, and she lifted the pin out again with her bare hands and placed it on the table in front of Edgar, where it gleamed in the lantern light.

Edgar's face showed its first trace of fear. "How is it that you, a human, can claim my eternal soul?"

"I am no human," she spat. "For centuries I have bartered in souls to prolong my life. A soul is the most sought-after currency on earth. Keep yours for now, Mr. Tripp. I can wait. But once you break the curse, it becomes mine to use as I please."

"I will not break the curse."

"Every soul returns to me eventually," she said with a wink. "You may keep your tongue as well, for you will need it to complete the spell." She pulled a long, slender dagger from a pouch at her side and traced the tip with one finger. "But you will return by week's end to settle your debt, or I will come to collect it myself." Her features began to change. Flesh blackened; teeth became sharp and rotted; limbs grew misshapen and impossibly thin.

I shut my eyes. I felt a tug on my hand, and suddenly we were back in John's house again.

"Yuck," I said with a shudder. "That was . . . educational." I met John's eyes, a plan already forming in my mind. "Did you know about the rule that he can't touch anyone or anything?"

"I did not, though I had my suspicions. This is the key to ending it for good, Josie. Well done."

I nodded. "I think I know what to do."

"I can tell you that he still loves Elsie, that he has always felt lonely and isolated. Yet he is arrogant, believing he can never be beaten. He will be there to watch the disaster unfold. He has not missed a single one. Perhaps this information will be of some help to you."

"Got it."

"Please forgive me, Josie. I did not mean to put you in

this position. You are a brave young lady, and you have two resourceful brothers to assist you."

"Thanks."

I waited awkwardly, not knowing how to say good-bye, but he simply nodded at me, his eyes solemn. "Good luck."

17

I WOKE WITH A GASP, RACKED WITH TREMORS, teeth chattering.

Mason was ready with a mountain of blankets. He wrestled them from the floor to my lap in one big heap.

Fox sat on the coffee table, watching me closely. "How'd it go?"

I sat, shivering and half aware, but I felt a smile tug at my face. For the first time in what felt like forever, I knew what to do.

"He can't touch anyone or anything," I said. "If he does, the curse is broken."

"How does that help us?"

"We're going to make him so angry that he breaks the curse himself. I need to dig up more ammunition, though. As soon as I can get my fingers working again." I blew into my cold-stiffened hands, trying to still their trembling.

We switched on the TV again while I pulled myself together.

The first thing we saw was a picture of Uncle Bill in the corner of the screen. "More than a dozen arrests have been made since the first Mothman sighting yesterday, mostly involving charges of trespassing or destruction of public property. But the most notable of those is local businessman Bill Reevey, an employee of Fletcher Auctions who was arrested today on suspicion of orchestrating the recent rash of sightings . . ."

I moved to turn the channel, but Fox stopped me. "I want to see this."

But they'd already moved on to the next segment. A reporter stood in front of the Field House, where a huge crowd had gathered. Some of them were protesters, marching with signs declaring, WE BELIEVE! and BEWARE THE MOTH and even THE END IS NEAR.

Another group carried signs saying things like, GET A LIFE and BUGS ARE PEOPLE, TOO, and THE TRUTH WILL SET YOU FREE. The two groups kept shouting insults at each other.

A third group seemed to be early tailgaters, supporters of the two high school teams slated to play in the championship game. They wore either the red and black of the Rebels or the green and gold of the Bulldogs, and they didn't shout at each other so much as just made a lot of noise in general.

"What are all those people doing there?" I demanded, sitting up. "Do we have to save them, too?"

We heard a car pull up out front. Mason ran to the front window. "It's Aunt Barb!"

"Is Uncle Bill with her?" Fox said.

"No."

When Barb walked in, she was calm on the outside, but on the inside I could tell a mighty storm was brewing.

"You wouldn't believe the things they're saying," she said in greeting, shaking her head. "Bail is set at $20,000. It's madness. Your uncle, the Mothman mastermind. Of all people," she huffed. "They can't prove a dang thing and they know it. The worst thing he's ever done in his life is forget to pay the parking meter."

"On the news there were a bunch of new Mothman sightings. Real ones," Fox said. "And Uncle Bill was in jail when they happened. Doesn't that prove that he's innocent?"

"You'd think so. There's just all this red tape to work through, and some nonsense about vandalism at the Field House."

I bit my lip. So did Fox. So did Mason. Barb saw me on the couch, buried under the mound of blankets and pillows. "Josie, are you still not feeling well?" She felt my forehead. "You feel like a Popsicle."

"I'm okay."

"Let me make you some tea. Have you all had lunch? I brought burgers. Just came home to shower, then it's back to the station. I'd rather not have to raise bail money if I can help it," she rambled.

"What about Dad?" Mason said.

"I've been on the phone with him off and on this morning. He's still doing fine, but we agree it's better for him to stay at the hospital for one more day, with all this craziness going on."

"Aw," Mason said, slumping down in the pile of pillows.

She smoothed a lock of hair from Mason's forehead. "He said to tell you all that he loves you, and he'll be home real soon."

I squeezed my eyes shut, willing myself not to sink into a pity party. I crawled out of my nest of blankets to eat the food she brought, though I couldn't even taste it. Even the boys picked at their burgers and fries.

When Aunt Barb left again, I knew we had to get moving on a plan.

"Fox, how many ideas did you guys come up with for tomorrow?"

"Four or five."

"I want you to keep going until you have thirty ideas on that list. Can you do that?"

"Thirty?" he said. "Why so many?"

"Humor me."

"What will you be doing, Josie?" Mason asked.

"Research."

* * *

Two hours later we met in the kitchen to compare notes.

"Is there a pet store in town that sells bats?" I said.

"Bats?" Fox said.

"Never mind. I'll call about it in a little while."

"Oookay."

Fox had grabbed the Field House plans from the Cave and spread them out on the kitchen table. "The quilt show goes from ten to three tomorrow," I said, "with setup starting at eight. The game is at seven p.m. They start letting players and concessions workers in at three thirty through the back entrance."

"First things first," Fox interrupted. "How do we break the curse, Josie? Tell me you have that worked out. How do we know Mothman will even show up?"

"I'm counting on it. John said Edgar always shows up to watch the disaster in person. It's horrible, I know. But this time it will help us. I need him there if my plan is going to work."

"How are you going to make him mad?" Mason said.

"I could use your help with that, actually. We need to dream up as many insults about Edgar as we can think of."

Their faces brightened. They took turns rattling them off almost faster than I could write them down. Then I used my cell phone to record myself reading them out loud.

"So, do you guys have your list?"

"Yes, but first I thought of another problem," Fox said. "What if we end up *causing* the thing we're trying to prevent? Like, what if we're trying to clear the building and we start a stampede or something?"

"Good thinking," I said. "We'll have to be extra careful about the plan we choose."

He dropped a piece of notebook paper on the table with a flourish and a courtly bow. "Here you are, then. Thirty ideas for emptying the Field House, ranging from improbable to pretty much impossible."

"The bees were my idea," Mason said.

I started at the top, reading each proposal out loud:

1. Flood
2. Fire—real or imaginary
3. Gas leak—imaginary
4. Stink bombs
5. Smoke bombs
6. Prison break—imaginary
7. Escaped zoo animals—real or imaginary
8. Power outage
9. Plumbing outage
10. Swarm of bees
11. Nuclear reactor leak—imaginary
12. Food poisoning
13. Steal and/or pop all the basketballs
14. Padlock all the doors before anyone can get in
15. Blast really annoying music
16. Hypnotize the crowd
17. Bribe people to leave

I stopped reading and glared at Fox across the table. "How are we gonna bribe five thousand people to leave the arena?"

"Hey, you said come up with thirty ideas. You didn't say they had to be good."

"Fair enough." I sighed and kept reading. But the ideas got worse from there. I tried to hide my disappointment, but Fox wasn't fooled.

"It's a pretty awful list, I know," Fox said. "I warned you."

"No, no, I think we can work with some of these."

"I put a star next to the ones that actually seemed doable."

I nodded my agreement, circling the one I liked best. "It's a great list. Creative. Good job, guys. Let's start with the power outage. I don't know how to do that." I stared at Fox. "Do you?"

"Not yet," Fox said. "But that's why we have the Internet, right?"

Mason's eyes gleamed. "We'll wreck the power so good it'll take them days to fix it."

"Whoa, what do you mean, 'we,' short stuff?" I said. "You're not coming, Mason."

He jumped to his feet. "Why not?"

"Are you kidding?" I said. "Fox, did you tell him he could come tomorrow?"

"I, uh, might have mentioned it when he was helping with the list."

"No way. I don't want him anywhere near that building tomorrow. Sorry, Mason."

"You're not Momma!" he shouted, face red. "You can't tell us what to do!"

He ran upstairs to his room. I wrapped my arms across my stomach, feeling like I'd been punched.

"Josie, he's seven," Fox said quietly. "He didn't mean it. In half an hour, he'll forget all about it."

"I know." I tried to shake off Mason's outburst, knowing there were more important things to worry about. "Okay, so, you wreck the power. Then what?"

"Everyone sits in the dark for a while," Fox explained. "The people in charge figure out there's nothing they can do, so they cancel the game and calmly escort everyone from the building."

"Sounds good in theory," I said. "Let's do it."

We moved to the study to search for information about large-scale power outages. Fox did the typing while I watched over his shoulder. "It has to be something they can't fix in a couple of minutes," I said.

"Can't we just cut some wires?" Fox said.

"If you're sure you won't electrocute yourself."

"Right. I'll keep looking, then."

I wandered around the study, thinking about the protesters and tailgaters we'd seen on TV. "I'm worried about all the people outside the Field House," I told Fox. "Couldn't they get hurt, too?"

"I guess, but what are we supposed to do about it? We can't be everywhere at once," Fox said.

"You're right. That's why I think we need more manpower."

"Well, with Mason out of the picture, that just leaves

me and you. What are we supposed to do, recruit people? Who on earth will even listen to us?" Fox said. Before I could answer, he sat up and snapped his fingers. "Wait, I think I know."

"Who?"

"We've got Dad's computer right here along with his entire customer e-mail list. A bunch of them are big, strong farmer types. I'll bet they'd help."

A dozen reasons why it wouldn't work hovered on the tip of my tongue, but I bit them back. *Why not?* "Okay."

Together, we composed an e-mail promising fifty of Dad's best customers an exclusive, up-close, in-depth preview of previously unseen Goodrich estate items, but only if they could be at our house within the next hour.

"Most of them will come if they can," Fox said as he pressed Send. "Then all we have to do is convince them that the city is in danger and that we're not a family of big, fat liars. Easy."

We waited. The minutes dragged by, impossibly long. Finally, cars started pulling into the long gravel driveway. When Mason saw all the activity outside his window, he hurried downstairs to get in on the action, acting as if all was forgiven.

Brothers Carl and Joe, who lived a half mile down the

road, got there first. We set up chairs on the auction floor and sat people down to wait, figuring it made more sense to explain everything once instead of over and over as they trickled in. We hoped it would also make them less likely to storm off in a huff when they heard what we had to say.

We gave everyone an hour; after thirty minutes, we already had thirty-seven people sitting there looking antsy. Mason served sodas and lemonade to keep them happy.

Carl shuffled over to where Fox and I were greeting people at the door. "They come to their senses and let your uncle out yet?"

"Not yet," I said.

He looked around. "Where's your aunt? She did authorize all this, right?"

"She's at the police station trying to get Uncle Bill released," Fox said.

"Then who the heck is running this thing?"

"I am." Fox glanced at me and quickly corrected himself. "We are."

"Your dad know about this?"

"Of course. It was his idea."

Carl stared at Fox a long while. He clicked his tongue. "Uh-huh," he said at last. But he didn't go home. He found a chair front and center and sat himself down to wait. We had roughly the same conversation a dozen more times with many of the new arrivals.

At last it was 3:00 p.m. Fox stepped up to the podium microphone and cleared his throat.

"Uh, hello and thank you for coming."

"What, no sideshow today? Where's the moth?" someone called out, causing a wave of laughter to ripple across the crowd.

"I promise all of you we will honor our word to give you first preview of the new Goodrich items."

"That's why we're here, kid," another person said.

"But *first*, we need you to listen to us for five minutes."

Grumbles started up immediately.

I stepped forward. "Just five minutes. Please. Most of you have been coming to Fletcher Auctions since before we were born. You know our family; you know we're honest and fair. Maybe you believe that our uncle faked those Mothman sightings to help business. Hopefully you know he would never do such a thing. But right now the most important thing you need to know is that a lot of people are in danger, and we need your help to save them."

"What kind of danger?"

"We're, uh, not totally sure, but it's going to happen tomorrow at the Field House," I said.

"You mean those threats painted on the side of the building? It was vandalism, pure and simple."

Someone else stood. "Unless you're trying to tell us your family had something to do with that."

"No. *Listen*," I begged. "We have a reliable tip that something's going to happen to the building, putting hundreds or even thousands of people in danger!"

A couple of people stood up to leave.

"Hear them out," someone shouted.

"Why? They're obviously behind this whole mess. They got their uncle thrown in jail. I want no part of it." The man plus three others left without looking back.

"You have to believe us," Fox insisted. "Why would we lie about something like this?"

"Come on now, Fox," Carl said. "Everyone knows you got to have all eyes on you whenever possible."

"There are no cameras here—just us," Fox said. "All we want to do is save lives."

Mr. Leonard from the drugstore spoke up. "Tell the police."

"They already think this is all a big scam. You're all we have left," I said.

"So we're supposed to put ourselves in danger, too, smack in the middle of some mysterious disaster?" Mr. Leonard said. "No, thank you."

Five more people got up and left.

One of the few women there spoke up. "If what you

say is really true, why should we risk ourselves? We have our own families to think of."

"Okay," I said. "Think about your families, then. What if your kids or grandbabies or wife or husband were in there, unsuspecting? Wouldn't you want someone to help them if they could?"

"How do you know something's going to happen? Did Mothman tell you?"

"John Goodrich did," I said.

That got them quiet.

"His wife was supposed to stop the Clark landslide, or at least warn people to leave," Fox said. "Now he's trying to help us stop another awful disaster."

Chairs slid back, scraping against the concrete floor. Half the room stood up to leave. Then Carl stood, his bulk and height and steely gray stare shaming them into sitting back down.

"We lived in Clark," he said. "I remember, Goodrich and his wife, they said things, did things—crazy things, telling people they were in danger. These were respectable people and one day they just went off the rails. Then the moth started showing up."

We heard several gasps.

"We listened. Me and Joe and our wives and kids—we left town and we're all alive because of it. I owe the Goodrich family my life. A lot of folks chose not to listen and died as a result. If people in Athens are in danger, I owe them my help. What do you need us to do?"

We looked around the room. Eight people remained— including Carl and Joe. My heart unclenched just a tiny bit knowing we had a few allies on our side.

"Here's the plan."

18

THE CUSTOMERS LEFT ONE BY ONE, PLEDGING their help. I asked Carl and Joe to stay behind for a minute.

"Do either of you know where I can get some bats?"

"Bats?" Carl echoed.

"You know, bats? They're fuzzy and they fly around at night, and they make these ultrasonic sounds to help them catch bugs. Do you know where I can get some? I called animal control, but apparently they don't just give bats to anyone who wants them."

"You looking to keep a pet? You're better off with a parakeet," Carl said.

Joe clapped his brother on the back. "She doesn't want them for pets, you thickheaded half-wit."

Carl lifted his trucker hat to scratch his head. "Matter of fact, my neighbor works for animal control. Been there twenty years. Got the scars to prove it."

"Really? Wow, that's a stroke of good luck right there," I said. "Dad always says you and Joe are our very best customers, and good people besides. Always willing to do a favor for someone in need."

"I'd like to think so."

"So this neighbor, he's a close friend? He might be able to pull a few strings if you asked him? One quick phone call would sure be a big help to us, if it's not too much trouble, of course."

Joe chuckled. "Been taking lessons from your brother, have you? He'd be happy to make a call for you, Josie. Wouldn't you, Carl?"

He huffed and grumbled. "I suppose you need me to bring them in the morning?"

"Yes, that would be perfect! Thank you!"

We walked them out to the lot where Joe's truck was parked. I couldn't believe what I saw stenciled on the driver's side door. "Joe, you're an electrician?"

"Yes, I am."

"Would you mind if Fox asked you a few questions?"

* * *

Aunt Barb came home alone around six o'clock. She didn't say much, but her eyes were red from crying. We helped with dinner, brought her coziest slippers, and put her favorite movie in the DVD player before sneaking back to Dad's study. When I peeked in on her an hour later, she was fast asleep.

Fox and I didn't sleep that night.

We pored over maps and schedules, walked through our current plan, and tossed around a few new ones. We read up on security systems and fire alarms and public PA systems.

Each of us loaded up a backpack with supplies. One of the perks of Dad's business was that we had access to pretty much anything we could possibly need. Fox packed wire cutters, fireworks, two sets of walkie-talkies with extra batteries, and a set of lock picks he'd scrounged from who-knows-where. "Do you even know how to use those?" I asked him.

"It can't be that hard," he answered.

I brought a tool kit, a portable power source the size of a loaf of bread, trail mix and bottles of water, my cell phone, a photograph of Elsie I'd printed from the Internet—and my picture of Momma, for courage.

Around five in the morning, I wrote a note for Aunt Barb, hating to add to her stress but knowing it was better than just leaving without a word. It said, *We had something really important to take care of today. We'll be fine. Try not to worry.*

Next I kissed Mason goodbye. Luckily he was still asleep, sprawled across his bed clutching his stuffed alligator.

Fox ruffled his hair and left an old handheld electronic football game on his nightstand as a peace offering.

A quick check of the morning news showed that plenty of people were still milling around outside the Field House. But we also got an unexpected piece of good news.

"Quilt show's been canceled," Fox announced, checking the Field House website for confirmation. "With all the crazies camped out there and the threats flying around, the organizers decided to reschedule."

"That's great," I breathed.

"The building will be mostly empty until this afternoon," Fox said.

"Let's still go over this morning like we planned, just to make sure we're ready."

Fox told me he'd taken care of our transportation, but I was still surprised when a cab pulled up out front.

"When did you have time to call a cab?"

"Last night."

"I'm surprised you didn't get a limo."

"Have to keep a low profile," he said, voice colored with regret. "Plus the limo couldn't come on such short notice. You have the pin?"

I patted the moth pin on my collar and nodded.

As we stepped outside, the wind whipped our hair and stung our faces. A bank of steely gray clouds hovered off to the west. Most of the cow pasture crowd had thinned, but enough people remained to notice our presence. A man with a microphone stood in front of a news truck giving a report. As soon as he saw us come out, he rushed over, microphone first.

"It's Fox Fletcher with his little sister! Tell us, how do you feel about your uncle being arrested? Did he ask you to fake Mothman sightings for him? Did your father fake breaking his leg in order to gain sympathy?"

Fox paused on his way to the taxi, ready to serve up some sharp-tongued reply, but I opened the back door of the taxi, shoved him in, and turned to face the camera just long enough to shout, *"I'm older! And it's*

Josie Fletcher, J-O-S-I-E." I got in the car and slammed the door.

"Go!" Fox told the driver as more people started to surround the car.

The driver spun the tires in the gravel as we shot out of the driveway. He grinned over the seat at us. "I've always wanted to do that," he said. "This place, your family, you're all over the news. You think I'll be on TV, too?" His grin faltered when he saw that it was just the two of us. "Wait, there's no adult with you? I don't want to get in trouble for taking you somewhere you're not supposed to be."

"We paid in advance," Fox said calmly. "Our dad arranged it."

"From the hospital?"

"Yep."

The driver checked his invoice and nodded. "Okay. You going to visit him, then?"

"Nope. The Field House, please."

"A little early to be going to the game, isn't it?" We glanced sidelong at each other, scrambling to come up with a decent answer, but it turned out we didn't need one.

"Should be a good one," the guy rambled. "My brother's kid plays point guard for the Bulldogs. Which team are you cheering for?"

"The Bulldogs, definitely," Fox said. They talked on

and on about basketball and about sports in general. Fox wasn't much of a jock; he preferred "intellectual pursuits," as he liked to say. But he also seemed to know just enough to carry on a conversation about almost anything, so he and the driver talked the whole way about pick and rolls and zone defense.

I let it all wash over me as I thought again about the ways the people at the Field House might be in danger. Short of someone planning something intentional, I could only think it would have to be some sort of fire or gas explosion. Fox's idea of a stampede didn't sound impossible, either. I still couldn't shake the worry that we might end up causing the disaster instead of preventing it. I gazed out at the surly sky, mind racing.

Fox tipped the driver ten dollars when we got there.

"Where are you getting all this money?" I whispered. "Have you been stashing it on the side?" The look on his face said it all. "You have!"

Fox shrugged. "Good thing I did, don't you think?"

"I'm still mad," I told him.

We found a quiet corner not far from where I'd spray-painted *BEWARE* on the wall just two days before. It was still there.

The spot gave us a good view of the tunnel entrance for players, performers, and employees. That's where we met up with Carl, Joe, and the other customers who'd agreed to help.

Most of them had made picket signs like we'd asked, so they could blend in with the groups of protesters and keep an eye on things from the outside. I recognized a few key phrases I'd requested, including MOTHMAN = MURDERER and EDGAR, KISS YOUR SOUL GOODBYE.

They were all there, even though it was early and cold, a drizzling rain clinging to our clothes. I looked into their faces—some we barely knew, others who'd known us our whole lives—and felt a rush of gratitude.

Carl stood holding a small cage with a towel draped over it. "Your bats, madam."

I peeked under the towel to see three sleeping bats dangling from a long, thin branch.

"Thank you."

Fox handed him a walkie-talkie in return and designated him point man for the group outside. "Channel three."

"What if we run into somebody we know?" someone asked.

"Just tell them you're a basketball fan. Or an anti-Mothman activist. Just make something up," Fox said.

"Some of us aren't as good at it as you," Carl said.

Over the next hour, the crowd swelled as fans and

protesters arrived by the carload. The number of police and security guards grew, too. But there was no sign of Mothman.

We kept a close eye on the lower-level entrance. It took a while, but finally the door opened. A janitor wheeled out a cart piled with bags of trash. The door swung shut behind him. Fox and I hurried down a concrete ramp and hid behind a corner thirty feet from the door. Fox crouched down like a runner at the starting blocks. The janitor returned from dumping the trash, opened the door with his ring of keys, and maneuvered his cart through. Fox took off running, catching the door with his toe just before it slammed shut.

I trotted after him, and together we slipped inside the Field House. We found ourselves in a maze of gloomy concrete tunnels beneath the arena.

Our first stop was the announcer's booth on the second level, so we could get a look at the audio system.

"You remember the way?" Fox said.

I nodded and started walking. We came to a T intersection, and I had to pause to get my bearings. Was it right or left? I closed my eyes and pictured the map we'd memorized.

"Left," I said, and took off walking again.

We found a bank of elevators but decided it would be safer to use the stairs. We expected security to be light so early in the morning, but you could never be too careful.

Since Fox's lock picks were mostly just for show, I was glad that when we arrived at the announcer's booth, it was unlocked and empty.

We looked down at the stands and the court below. Fox whistled. "This place is a lot bigger in person."

We stared at the dizzying number of buttons and knobs on the media console. "Don't touch anything," I warned.

"Don't worry," Fox said.

"We just need a microphone, right? How hard can that be?"

We climbed beneath the console, following various power cords back to their source. Once we found one attached to a microphone, we marked it with a red X.

"With the power out, you'll have to plug this into the portable battery."

"Got it."

"Can you get up here fast enough after you cut the power? How are you going to get past the announcers when the time comes?"

"Quit worrying. I'll be fine," Fox said.

"Hiding spot next?" I said.

"Yep. Storage closet fourteen-B on the main level."

We'd picked a central location where Fox could get to the lower level within a minute or two. But when we got to the closet, the door was locked.

"They lock up the toilet paper but not the media equipment? Weird."

"Why don't we just go knock out the power right now?" I said. "Get it over with."

"We talked about this," Fox said. "We have to wait for Mothman to show so you can get him to break the curse. If we stop the disaster too soon . . . "

"I know. It won't end well for me. Mothman has to break the curse before we do."

"The timing's going to be tricky," Fox said. "At the first sign of Mothman, we have to be ready to move." Fox jiggled the doorknob once more. "Lock picks?" he said.

I shrugged. "I'd love to see you try."

I kept watch for security guards and random passersby while Fox tried his best, but after ten minutes, he'd gotten nowhere. "Looks like we'll have to choose a new hiding spot."

"Can I try?" I said.

"Knock yourself out."

I hefted the tools to get a feel for them, running my fingers over each delicate tip. Sometimes I used a tiny set of tools to repair pieces of jewelry Dad gave me; these didn't feel too different. I stuck one into the keyhole, closed my eyes, and threaded the tool by touch and sound. I felt one tumbler move, then another, and then, with a gentle click, the lock released and the door opened.

I smiled. "Beginner's luck," I said with only a hint of smugness.

Fox walked past without a word, though I caught him stealing curious glances my way.

We made ourselves comfortable in the tiny space. I set the cage down in one corner.

Around 10:00 a.m., Fox checked in with Carl. "How's it going out there?"

"My feet hurt," Carl said. "And I'm tired of getting into arguments with people over Mothman."

"You're doing great," Fox told him. "Hang in there."

Hours passed with no sign of Mothman. The pin remained dormant. We kept track of how many people walked past by the number of feet we saw through the crack beneath the door. We snacked. We watched the bats sleep.

Carl radioed us around three o'clock to say: "Team buses just pulled up."

"Thanks, Carl."

We blew through all our snacks and water by late afternoon. After a bathroom break at six thirty, Fox returned to tell me the teams were warming up on the court. The number of feet milling past the door was mounting by the minute.

We started arguing about the timing of our plan.

"I'm worried. It's getting late," I said. "Where is he? If we wait too long, we won't have enough time to get everyone out. Maybe John was wrong. Maybe Mothman isn't going to show."

"It's all a guessing game at this point," Fox said. "We could always forget the power and just pull the fire alarm as soon as he shows."

"Then people will have two reasons to panic. They'll trample each other."

"What do you suggest, then?"

"I think you should go ahead and cut the power now."

"Josie . . ."

I risked a peek out the door. "We have to. Look at all these people, Fox! We have to."

He clenched his jaw but switched on his radio. "What's the chatter, Carl?"

"No Mothman. The rain's picking up, but the crowd hasn't thinned much."

"You're a rock. Looks like we're ready for Joe. Have him meet us at the north entrance, okay?"

"You sure?"

"Yeah," Fox said.

"Okay, then. He's on his way."

Fox turned to me. "Are you sure this is going to work, Josie?"

I swallowed around a sudden lump in my throat. "No."

"What? You promised me you had it all worked out."

"I'm scared, Fox."

"Yeah, me too." He stuffed his hands in his pockets. "So, have you picked the next person to be cursed? In case we fail, I mean? There's not much time left."

"Not yet," I said.

"If you don't . . ."

I swallowed. "I know. Mothman will probably pick someone I love."

"Pick me," Fox blurted.

"No! I can't do that, Fox."

"But we're practically experts at this now. I can handle it."

I wanted to slap the pretend-cocky smile off his face. "I won't pick someone, especially not you. Don't ask me to."

"If we fail, he'll pick Dad, or Uncle Bill, or Aunt Barb. *Or Mason.*"

"Shut up!" I shouted, clenching my fists. "I don't intend to fail. Are you coming?"

We gathered our stuff. I grabbed the cage and we abandoned our hiding spot for good. It was crowded enough that we could slip out into the concourse without attracting more than a few curious glances.

We met up with Joe, who had insisted on being present for any tampering with the power. We ducked into a nearby stairwell, down a flight of stairs, and through a winding maze of corridors, pausing every few minutes to listen for footsteps. At last we came to a set of double doors with the hum of heavy machinery behind them. The doors were painted bright red with a sign that read: WARNING: AUTHORIZED PERSONNEL ONLY. ALARM WILL SOUND.

I pulled some glow sticks from my backpack and handed them out.

"Give us about ten minutes, huh?" Fox said. "Then I'll hustle upstairs to the media booth."

I checked my phone for the time. "That should be right before tipoff. I'll go back upstairs and watch for Mothman."

Fox caught my arm, met my eye. "We'll see you soon."

I nodded.

I made my way back out to the main concourse, my footsteps heavy. Hundreds of people were milling around, smiling, laughing, buying souvenirs or food, checking their tickets against the signs overhead.

I felt the pin with my fingers for any trace of cold, but nothing had changed. As the tide of people flowed around me, I felt like I was stuck in slow motion, underwater, as if time itself had shifted. Someone jostled my arm; two people bumped into the cage as they passed. I ducked out of the path of several rowdy teenagers and collided with a huge man carrying nachos and a sixty-four-ounce soda.

"Josie?"

It was Mitch.

He stared down at me. "What are you doing here?" His gaze traveled to my backpack, his eyes narrowing. "Please tell me you're not still carrying on with this Mothman stuff."

"I don't have time for this," I said, pushing past him.

Mitch followed me, tossing his nachos and drink in the nearest trash can. "What are you planning?" His voice was getting too loud for comfort.

I pulled him aside, into a stairwell marked AUTHO-RIZED PERSONNEL ONLY.

"Look, we did the graffiti, okay? I admit it, but it was for a reason. Something bad really is going to happen tonight. Haven't you seen the news? Mothman is all over the place. This is real."

He shook his head. "I can't let you do this."

Helpless anger surged through me. "Haven't you done enough? I won't let you sabotage us when we've made it this far."

Mitch studied my face. "You really believe all these people are in danger, don't you?"

"Why else would we *be* here? Do you have any idea what I've been through this week, the things I've seen? I never wanted this, never wanted my family to get hurt. Now a lot of people are about to die, and I have a chance to change that. *Why would I lie?* Please, Mitch. *Please.*"

"If I can't change your mind . . ."

I held my breath, ready to bolt if I had to.

His expression changed, softened. "Then you'd better let me help you."

I eyed him suspiciously. "You can tag along if you want to, but you won't stop me."

"I guess I can live with that," he said.

Carl clicked through on the radio: "Weather's getting bad out here."

"Still no sign of Mothman?" I said.

"Nope. Nothing."

I checked my phone. Three minutes until Fox cut the power. "We need to get out in the open," I said to Mitch.

We crossed from the stairwell back into the main concourse. I could hear a booming voice announcing the teams' starting lineups to wild cheers of the crowd.

Mitch kept glancing around with a guilty look on his face.

"Quit it," I told him. "Just act natural. First thing I learned from Fox, like a decade ago, is that nobody will stop you if you act like you belong there. If you act shifty, people will know you're up to something."

"Excuse me."

I stopped short.

A security guard stood in front of us, arms folded across his chest.

19

"**D**ID I JUST SEE YOU COME OUT OF A restricted area?"

I glanced over my shoulder and pointed at the door behind us. "What, in there? Were we not supposed to be in there?" My efforts to look innocent were completely ruined by Mitch's bright red ears and fidgeting.

The guard ignored me. "And who are you, sir?"

"Um . . ."

"Are you aware that you were in an area that's off-limits? That I'll need to hold you for questioning? We've had a lot of weird stuff going on here this week—pranks, threats, you name it. We don't take that lightly."

Mitch opened his mouth to answer, and the lights went out.

The crowd went from cheers to hushed murmurs and gasps. It was pitch-dark for maybe ten seconds, then the exit signs winked back on, followed by emergency track lighting every ten feet or so along the base of the walls.

The guard hesitated and finally pointed at the two of

us. "Don't go anywhere." Then he strode off down the concourse.

"Nice timing, Fox," I whispered.

We made our way out to the bleachers. The players stood on the court, eyes glued to the ceiling as if the lights would come back on at any moment, their forms like ghostly silhouettes.

The crowd noise grew, people shuffling and murmuring and a few fans shouting out, "Yeah! Go Bulldogs!" or "Bulldogs suck! Go Rebels!"

No power meant no speaker system, just like we'd figured. Pretty soon a man with a megaphone came out onto the court. "Please, everyone, remain in your seats. We are looking into the problem and urge your patience and cooperation. Again, please remain in your seats and do not panic."

The lights blinked on suddenly, blindingly, to a chorus of cheers.

"Okay, folks, it looks like the backup generator is doing its—"

The lights winked out again. The crowd groaned.

The announcer gave a nervous laugh. "All right, then. Anyone know a good joke?"

Mitch and I cracked a few glow sticks and hung them around our necks. We stood in the near-dark for twenty minutes. High above us, glass skylights ran the length of the ceiling. We could see angry clouds looming, casting odd shadows each time they were lit by a flash of lightning. Mitch stayed by my side, tense and alert. I chewed my nails as the crowd grew more and more restless. How long would it take them to call the game and evacuate? If they'd found the source of the problem, they'd know by now that the lights wouldn't be on anytime soon.

At last, the announcer returned to the court. "All right, folks. Thank you for your patience. I'm afraid I've been informed that the power cannot be fixed this evening."

The crowd groaned and booed and stomped their feet. A few people shouted into the disappointed silence that followed.

"Rest assured the game will be rescheduled and all tickets honored. We ask that you gather your personal belongings and walk to the nearest exit, where Field House staff are standing by to assist you if needed."

It worked. It had actually worked! The building would be empty in a matter of minutes, and still no sign of—

The pin pulsed hot, then cold. I spun around, scanning the ceiling.

"Watch your step now, and please drive carefully," the announcer was saying. "We've had reports of some rough weather to the south . . . "

WHOOSH.

A shadowed figure swooped down from up near the scoreboard, down over the court, and back up to a far corner of the huge gymnasium, then took another pass just over the heads of the crowd, red eyes ablaze for all to see.

Beside me, Mitch froze, his eyes glued to the ceiling. Screams erupted all around the Field House. Children wailed. Fans scattered, pushing and shoving, running in all directions. They had to make it all the way down the bleachers to the floor to reach the exits. Several people fell as others tried to force them out of the way.

The exits began to bottleneck with people trying to escape.

I grabbed the walkie-talkie. "Fox, Code Red! Mothman's here."

"That's a ten-four," Fox said.

People scattered. Police officers and guards and ushers and even the man with the megaphone pled for calm. Mothman swooped again and again. His shape was an inky smear in the near-darkness, drawing fearful cries, feeding the chaos.

As I pressed through the crowd, Mitch saw me struggling and muscled in front of me just as I was nearly carried off my feet by a group of panicked high school kids. He grabbed my arm and pushed ahead, clearing a path.

I kept an eye trained on Mothman. Each time he would lunge down for another pass it was near one of the exits. People trying to leave would shrink back or dive for cover under the bleachers. Suddenly I understood. He was trying to make people stay, keep them trapped inside the gym. He paused over a cowering group of fans and turned his head in my direction, those red eyes boring into mine like the fires of hell.

I remembered the cage and fumbled for the door latch. Three furry shapes flew out into the arena, darting from perch to perch among the support beams with high-pitched squeaks, just visible in the glow of the emergency lights.

Mothman jerked. He spun around, scanning the rafters. He flinched and ducked aside every time the bats got near him. When one barely missed his head, he reached out and took a swing at it.

I held my breath—but Mothman pulled his arm back at the last second. The bat flew past untouched. I exhaled. So close.

It was now or never. "Fox, are you in position?" I said into the walkie-talkie, hoping he was manning his post in the announcer's booth, and that our power source worked.

I held up a picture of Elsie with her husband and children just as my recorded voice spilled from the loudspeakers overhead. "She's pretty, Edgar. Too bad she didn't want anything to do with you. She never loved you. Your curse didn't faze her. She ignored it, went on to live a happy life without giving you another thought. What does it feel like to be rejected your whole life? It's because people saw you for what you really are, like something on the bottom of a shoe. No remorse, no compassion. Don't you get it? You're more selfish than she ever was. Look at what you've become!" Even as my voice continued over the speakers, rattling off insults, another voice sounded in my head, vile and cold.

"*I'm giving these people a chance. That's more than*

they would have gotten if I'd never dreamed up the curse."

You're trying to keep them from leaving, I thought, confident he could hear every word. *Careful, Edgar. Isn't that against the rules?*

"*You think you can anger me enough to make me forget myself, to make me break the curse and risk my soul?*" His voice was a razor-sharp blade, a screw being turned inside my head. "*Others before you have tried and failed.*"

"You doomed your own soul when you made that deal!" I shouted aloud.

"*It is a fine effort, Josie, but you are already mine. You will not win.*"

Above the terrible noise of screams and running feet, my voice on the loudspeaker, and Mothman's voice in my head, a new sound rose, high and piercing. At first, I couldn't make sense of it, but realization dawned like a wave across the crowd.

Tornado siren.

People stopped running and pushing and stood still, eyes fixed on the glass skylights.

It wasn't a stampede, or a fire, or any other disaster we'd thought of. Just your run-of-the-mill, deadly tornado.

I grabbed up the walkie-talkie. "Carl?"

"We hear it!"

"How many people are still out there?"

"A few hundred."

"You have to get all those people *inside* the building, down to the tunnels. It's the safest place. You can't let them leave. Please! Do whatever it takes."

"We're on it."

I switched to Fox's channel. "Fox? Get down to the tunnels, right now, do you hear me? As fast as you can."

His face appeared in the window of the announcer's booth, looking down at the bleachers, trying to find me. "What about you, Josie?"

"I'll meet you there, okay? Okay? Tell me you understand me."

"I understand."

I jammed the radio back in my pocket. "The tunnels!" I cried out loud, but the only one who heard me was Mitch. He took up the call in his booming voice, and within seconds, word spread to the ushers and guards and the man with the megaphone. "Everyone!" the man shouted. "Use the exits and follow the ushers to the tunnels! Do not leave the building. Do not remain in the gymnasium. Please, head quickly and calmly to the tunnels and locker rooms and assist others around you."

Mothman was still focused on me, eyes burning in fury. Did that mean he felt threatened, that we actually had a chance?

"I will save them!" I screamed at him. There were still people trying to make their way down from the bleachers. "Mitch!" I shouted, pointing to a mother carrying a wailing toddler, struggling to keep hold of her. "Help me!"

We pushed, squeezed, and shimmied our way through the crowd to reach them. Mitch reached up and gathered the little girl into his arms. The woman's face was wet with tears. "What's happening?" she cried. "Is Mothman causing this? Is there really a tornado?"

"Yes," I told her. "You have to get underground."

At last, the crowds began to thin as people swarmed out of the gym and into the concourse. I could only hope they were being herded into the tunnels, or somewhere safer than where we were. I spotted a couple of boys younger than Mason, crying and huddled together. I took off in their direction. "Josie, wait!" Mitch called.

"Make sure they get out!" I said, nodding at the girl he still held.

I glanced around to see where Mothman had got to. He still hovered, watching and waiting. I knelt down beside the boys. "Have you lost your mom?"

The older one nodded. I stood and snagged the sleeve of the nearest person—a woman in her twenties shouting about losing her purse.

"Hey!" I shook her arm. "They need help!" I pointed

at the boys. The older one stood with his arm around the younger, his chin quivering.

"But my purse—"

"They can't find their mom and there's a tornado out there. You see those glass ceilings?" I pointed up. The woman nodded and swallowed. "You need to leave right now!"

She took the boys by their hands and ran for the exit.

"You know what I think hurts you the worst?" I shouted at Mothman. "That you're gonna get taken down by a twelve-year-old girl! We're winning—can't you see? These people are going to live, and you can't stand it, can you? Even if I die, at least the curse will be broken, and your soul is roadkill. You're finished, Edgar!"

I felt panic and denial rise within him.

The siren howled. The shouting and crying and pushing continued, though little by little the gym emptied. With the noise dying down, I could hear a new sound, a low rumbling, like a freight train gunning right for us.

"Josie!"

It was Fox, wearing his glow stick like a necktie, running toward me from the opposite side of the court fifty feet away. The rumbling grew. I could see Fox's lips moving but couldn't make out anything he was saying. Objects began pelting the roof, first what sounded like hail and then larger objects we could actually see:

branches, fence rails, jagged pieces of metal and wood. Cracks started appearing in the glass, spiderwebbing their way along the surface. The steel framework groaned.

I tore my eyes away. Fox's gaze was still locked on the ceiling. Even from so far away I could see the stark fear in his eyes. And he wasn't moving.

I tried to run toward him, but Mothman swept in front of me and hovered there, those fiery eyes so close I felt their heat singe my skin. I stopped short, tried to dart around him, but he rose up impossibly tall, wings a blur of constant motion, trapping me, making it impossible to see or move or think.

Edgar's voice crawled through my head. *"Even one life lost and the curse continues. Shall it be your brother? I can live with that."*

"Josie!" I could just make out Mitch's desperate voice calling my name.

"Get Fox!" I screamed. *"Please! Save Fox!"*

Mothman became darkness itself, smothering me from all sides, but still careful not to touch me. I fell to my knees, mouth gaping like a fish on land, desperate for air. Without sight or sound, all I could do was feel: *cold, despair, hate, envy, fear, loss—*

He would never break the curse on his own, I realized. But what if *I* touched *him*?

I reached out a trembling hand and grabbed hold of his robe.

"Noooo!" he shrieked.

Mothman shrank away from me. I gasped a few grateful breaths and tried to get my bearings.

Suddenly a pair of dress shoes stepped into my field of vision. I tried to force a warning from my burning throat, telling the fool to run—and then the shoes flickered.

John.

I stumbled to my feet and found Mothman and Goodrich staring each other down.

John's eyes were no longer sorrowful but piercing, furious, and focused on only Edgar.

Mothman reared up to his full height, eyes afire, but Goodrich didn't flinch.

"It's over, Edgar. The curse is broken."

I gasped. I could hear John even over the roaring winds, his voice clear and strong.

Hope filled me.

Mothman roared and raged. His figure loomed even larger, as black and grim as an empty grave.

John met my gaze. A half smile settled across his features, peace in his eyes. He glanced behind him as his wife's figure stepped up beside him and took his hand. Light blazed around them, bright as the winter sun, and they were gone.

Mothman howled. He rushed toward me, his clawed, crooked fingers stretching closer . . .

His form blurred as his wings and ragged black clothes began to shred and fall away. He stopped short, seeming to grasp that he was finished. Beaten.

Doomed.

We both looked up as the glass skylights burst and shattered, unleashing a torrent of rain, wind, glass, and chunks of ceiling. I glimpsed Edgar's cruel smile just before the last remnants of him vanished in a wisp of black smoke.

I had just enough time to throw my arms over my head before the world crashed down around me in a surge of noise and pain, knocking me off my feet. Debris pelted me, flaying my skin. Swallowing dirt and grit, I squeezed my eyes shut against the assault and started crawling, not knowing which direction to go.

Suddenly there was no floor beneath me. I grabbed desperately for anything to anchor me, caught something for a second, two seconds, until I was ripped away and flung into something hard and unyielding.

I felt a scream leave my throat, felt a white-hot pain in my leg—

—and then it all went away, the specter of red eyes following me into the darkness.

20

"JOSIE? JOSIE, CAN YOU HEAR ME?"

Sound came back first. Then pain. My head felt foggy and thick, like it was being squeezed by a giant hand. My ears were ringing, but that voice calling my name still got through, slightly muffled and sounding more distressed by the minute.

"Josie? *Please.* I can't tell Dad I let you get killed after we saved half the town. Wake up."

I managed to crack open my eyes and found myself staring at a clear, velvet sky salted with stars.

Fox's face appeared above mine, his eyes shining. "Oh, man. Oh, wow." He gulped a few long, slow breaths and scrubbed a hand across his forehead. "Oh, thank you. Hold still, okay?"

Huh?

Raw, angry pain pulsed through my leg. I turned my head to the side and saw a couple of paramedics or firefighter types kneeling beside me, strapping my leg to some kind of board, and then the screaming, gut-twisting,

mind-numbing pain came roaring up my leg and buzzing along every nerve.

"*Aaah!* Ow, ow, ow!" Tears sprang to my eyes. I
reached out desperately for anything to cling to and
found Fox's arm.

"Ow!" he cried. "Can't you give her a shot or something?"

"We just did. It should kick in soon."

"Make it stop, make it stop," I whimpered. I took another look at my leg and realized it was a lot puffier than
usual and also wanted to bend the wrong way.

"*Ugh.*" My stomach clenched and rolled, like ripples
in the water. My throat convulsed. I clamped a hand
over my mouth and tried desperately not to be sick.

"Try not to move, now," one of the paramedic guys
said. "Almost there. Then we'll get you transported."

Transported? I felt as if no one was making any sense.

"Why am I outside?" I whispered, my voice feeling
scratchy, like I'd swallowed a shovelful of dirt.

Fox smiled faintly. "Look again, Josie." I glanced past
him. The wooden floor beneath us was wet and filthy.
Just a few feet away were the remains of a row of bleachers, twisted and splintered, metal rods and poles sticking out at crazy angles. Kind of like my leg. I looked
away. On my other side, one of the basketball backboards
lay on its side, a shattered skeleton of itself.

The ceiling wasn't there anymore. Shards of glass lay everywhere, glittering in the huge spotlights that had been set up around the area.

As awareness grew I began to feel stinging cuts all over my body, and then I couldn't forget them, the pain surpassing even the solid mass of ache in my leg. I glanced at Fox again and saw his arms and face covered in tiny cuts, a few of them bandaged with little white strips.

"We're inside," I said stupidly. "Wait." I tried to sit up, but the pain made white sparkles dance in front of my eyes. "You said—" I winced and lowered myself back down. "You said we saved half the town. Did we do it? Is everybody okay?"

Fox grinned. "There are some injuries, but yes—we did it. No one died."

"And I'm alive?"

"Yeah. You are. How did you do it? Did Mothman touch you?"

"I touched him." I remembered the pin and felt for it at my collar, but it wasn't there.

Fox held out his clenched hand and slowly uncurled his fingers. The pin—or what was left of it—sat there, looking like nothing more than bits of glass and gold.

"Did you . . . ?"

"This was under your jacket when I found you."

I sighed. "Good."

I was starting to feel sleepy, my eyes heavy, the pain slipping away. "Mitch," I said, remembering. "Is he okay? Did he save you? I asked him to save you." *Ooh.* Floating. That was new.

"He did." Color rose in Fox's cheeks. "I froze. I remember seeing you, and seeing those cracks in the ceiling, and I couldn't think, couldn't move. Then the storm was inside instead of outside, and Mitch tackled me and dragged me out into the concourse. I kept trying to get back to you, and he wouldn't let me. I might have said a couple of words I shouldn't have."

I was drifting, too far gone to answer. Suddenly the sky got a little closer as they raised my stretcher to its full height.

"You riding with us, kid?" the paramedic asked someone. Fox, apparently, because he nodded and followed along.

* * *

The next time I woke up, I was in a hospital bed with Dad resting in a chair next to me, his casted leg propped up on a stool. My eyes drifted to my own leg, cocooned in a pink cast and resting on a plump pillow. I stared at it, marveling at the lack of pain, wondering how long it would take to heal.

"We're twins," Dad's voice said gently as he leaned over to kiss the top of my head. "How do you feel, honey?"

"I'm okay."

He placed a small device in my hand. "If the pain gets bad, you push that button, okay? It's medicine to help."

"The good stuff, huh?"

"Yeah. The good stuff." He closed his eyes, cleared his throat. "I'm so glad—" A tear dripped off the end of his nose, and then another. "I'm so glad that you're okay, Josie Bug. I should have been there with you."

"But we did it."

"I know you did. You saved *so many* people. I'm so proud of you."

The relief was so great I thought I might cry, but the tears wouldn't come. "How much do you know?"

"Fox told me some things about Mothman and a curse that curled my toes. But I have a feeling he left a whole lot out."

"Do people know what really happened?"

"Most think it was just a stroke of good luck that the power went out when it did, that people started to evacuate before the tornado hit."

"But Mothman, the warnings—some people must suspect something weird."

"Some do. The news is still giving him plenty of air-time, but most people are more concerned with the cleanup effort. Several of my customers sure think the world of you." I looked around the room for the first time and noticed vases of flowers, balloon bouquets, and assorted stuffed animals. I nestled back into the pillows. "Where's Fox and Mason? Are they okay?"

"I sent them down to the vending machines for a break. They're pretty wiped out."

"How about Mitch? He saved Fox, you know."

Dad's eyebrows lifted. "He did? Remind me to give him a raise, huh?"

"What about the town?" I said.

"The Field House took the worst of it. A few other buildings on campus were damaged, but luckily they were empty because of spring break. Most neighbor-hoods were spared, but several families lost their homes."

"That's so sad. What about—" *Huh. Strange.* Some-how my question didn't seem nearly as important as closing my eyes at the moment.

"Want to sleep a little more?"

"Yeah."

"Okay." He kissed me again and struggled to his feet, reaching for his crutches.

He hobbled out. I lay very still, listening to my

breath go in and out, staring at the perfectly intact and ordinary ceiling.

After a little while, the door opened and Fox crept in, carrying a cup of red Jell-O. I pretended to be asleep to see what he'd do.

He sat down in Dad's empty chair and managed to sit still for maybe two whole minutes. Then he started tapping his feet on the floor and drumming his fingers on the arms of the chair. Two more minutes and he had the TV on as loud as it would go.

"Do you mind?" I said at last, turning my head to face him.

"I knew you weren't asleep," he said, switching on the overhead light. I squinted at him with as much venom as I could muster.

"What do you want?"

"Nothing. I just came to bring you some Jell-O."

"You ate it." The empty cup sat on the bedside table, a few red glops still clinging to the rim.

"I can get you another one."

"Forget it."

"So . . . how you feeling?" he said.

I shrugged. "Tired. Can't feel much else."

"That's good."

"Yeah."

"Hey, Fox?"

"Yeah?"

Oh, good. Now the tears were starting. It took me three tries to get the words out through my traitorous throat.

"Thanks. For sticking by me. For everything."

He looked away, embarrassed. "I didn't do much. I wanted to burn down the Field House, remember? You were like . . . the Mothman whisperer. I've never seen anything so brave."

"I messed up every step of the way. A lot of it was just dumb luck. I'll never be like you."

"Me? What are you talking about? Do you have any idea what you just did?" He jumped up and started pacing. "You saved thousands of people and brought down a curse that's been around for more than a hundred years. Sure, you had some help. But people want to help you because you're *you*. You've always been like that. You keep our crazy family from falling apart."

"But Aunt Barb . . . " I said.

"No. *You*. When Momma died, I wasn't sure if we'd be okay, but you . . . you're the one who keeps us all sane. You don't ever give up. You're just as stubborn as she was. You even remind me of her sometimes."

"I do?"

He picked up the empty Jell-O cup and rolled it around in his hands. "You should talk to Dad about this stuff, or Aunt Barb, or, I don't know, a *therapist*. You're not supposed to burden your little brother with meaning-of-life stuff."

"I'm sorry."

He sighed dramatically. "I guess if I'm not permanently scarred by Mothman or by narrowly escaping a natural disaster, then I'll survive."

"Hey, Fox?"

"Yeah?"

"Do you miss her?"

"Of course I do. Every single day." He cleared his throat. After a few awkward seconds, the cocky smile was back on his face. "So you wouldn't believe all the media types in Athens right now. Think of the money we could make selling our story to the tabloids. Maybe even a book deal." He gave a happy sigh.

"Forget it. There's no way we're using this to make money, you con artist."

He looked offended. "You've gotten awfully bossy lately. What's up with that?"

I closed my eyes and smiled. "I'm older."

* * *

Uncle Bill came home that same day. Mitch withdrew his statement and the police dropped all the charges. It probably helped that everyone was so relieved about escaping the tornado that they forgot to be upset about the vandalism. A few witnesses and die-hard believers gave interviews, wrote letters to the editor, and camped out in the cow pasture for weeks waiting for Mothman's return. But most people convinced themselves the sightings had been a skillful hoax or mass delusion.

Mothman himself had disappeared. The remains of the pin were scattered in the wreckage of the Field House.

Every penny from the Goodrich auction—including Dad's thirty percent—went toward helping the town rebuild after the tornado.

A few months went by. We were glad to move on.

As a family treat, we loaded up the car and spent a week in Columbus at the state fair. There was still the matter of a junior bid call competition to see to.

Fox, of course, won the whole thing.

We walked around the fairgrounds afterward, browsing the flea market for cheap trinkets Fox could add to his haunted auctions. Fox carried his trophy around like a baby, bragging to anyone misguided enough to ask about it.

Mason clutched a cloud of cotton candy on a paper cone, leaving a sticky trail on everything he touched. A ring of blue sugar outlined his mile-wide grin.

Dad lugged around the giant stuffed dog that I won all on my own, playing ring toss.

In honor of Momma, Aunt Barb entered apricot jam in the fair and won first prize. She glowed with a pride to rival Fox's own. She and Uncle Bill held hands as they sampled fried Oreos and elephant ears from the snack vendors.

We stopped at a table filled with old skeleton keys, circus posters, and things in jars I didn't dare look at too closely. Fox picked up a huge, old magnifying glass, the bone handle carved with delicate flowers and twisting vines.

The stall owner raised an eyebrow at Fox's choice. "Ah, now, that's a special piece, not for the faint of heart." He dropped his voice to a tantalizing whisper. "That piece there, my boy, is haunted."

I groaned and Fox grinned, green eyes agleam. "You don't say."

AUTHOR'S NOTE

When I first started writing Josie and Fox's story, I knew I wanted it to be set at an auction house in Athens, Ohio. But I didn't know it would focus on the Mothman legend until a well-timed trip to the library. I went searching for books on ghosts and other supernatural creatures. There, on a display right by the front desk, was John A. Keel's *The Mothman Prophecies*. As soon as I started reading, I knew Mothman was the monster for me, especially when I learned that the town where he became famous—Point Pleasant, West Virginia—was just forty miles from Athens.

Opinions vary on when the first official Mothman sighting took place, but the first one to make the newspaper happened on November 15, 1966. Two couples driving near an abandoned explosives plant reported seeing a man with wings and fiery red eyes who took flight and chased their car at speeds close to 100 miles per hour.

The headline in the November 16 *Point Pleasant Register* read: COUPLES SEE MAN-SIZED BIRD...CREATURE...SOMETHING. Forty miles away, the *Athens Messenger* reported:

WINGED, RED-EYED 'THING' CHASES POINT COUPLES ACROSS COUNTRYSIDE.

The story spread, and the number of sightings swelled. People from all over the country traveled to Point Pleasant, hoping to spot the mysterious creature. Some sources claimed that Mothman appeared a hundred times or more over the next thirteen months. Others said the culprit was actually a large, red-crested bird called the sandhill crane. And, of course, hoaxes probably played a role. One of the more creative tricks I read about involved pranksters tying red flashlights to helium balloons.

Mothman earned his name from a reporter who compared him to a character from the 1960s *Batman* television series. Eyewitnesses didn't always agree on what Mothman looked like, but the most common traits were red eyes, leathery wings, and a height of seven to nine feet.

Mothman sightings had been tapering off by December 15, 1967, when the Silver Bridge, connecting Point Pleasant, West Virginia, and Kanauga, Ohio, collapsed during rush hour traffic, killing forty-six people. The link between the disaster and the sightings was first suggested by Gray Barker in his 1970 book, *The Silver Bridge*. Mothman gained a reputation as an unlucky omen—a promise of bad things to come. Did Mothman cause the tragedy? Or had he been trying to send a warning? Speculation swirled and the legend grew.

Mothman is a relative newcomer to American folklore, earning a place among legendary creatures such as Sasquatch and the Jersey Devil. His real moment in the spotlight came with the 2002 movie *The Mothman Prophecies*, based on John Keel's 1975 book. Because Mothman's origins are largely unexplored, I had the chance to create a backstory for him, shaping his role in the modern-day tale of three kids, a gold stickpin, and a deadly curse. I imagined that he had once been a man, someone who abandoned his humanity in favor of a twisted experiment to prove that there are no selfless people in the world. Thankfully, the Fletcher kids are there to set him straight. The pin and curse are my own inventions, though I do own a real moth stickpin that served as a handy (and creepy) source of inspiration. I also dreamed up the OU Field House (or at least this particular version of it) and the ill-fated town of Clark, Ohio, for my own nefarious purposes.

Point Pleasant has embraced the legend as its own. The town now hosts the Mothman Festival every September, and is home to a Mothman museum and a life-size Mothman statue.

If you'd like to know more about Mothman, check out these books, papers, and websites:

The Mothman Prophecies, by John Keel (Tor Books, 2013).

"How and Why Did the Mothman Come into Being?," Andrew Jay Harvey, www.academia.edu/542721/How _and_why_did_the_Mothman_come_into_being.

"The Mothman: A Folkloric Perspective," Corey J. Chimko, www.coreychimko.com/The_Mothman_A_Folk loric_Perspective.pdf.

"American Hauntings," prairieghosts.com.

"Mysterious Universe," mysteriousuniverse.org/?s= mothman.

ACKNOWLEDGMENTS

Thank you to Bryce, Nathan, Cam, and Nat for your incredible patience, love, and encouraging words.

Thank you to Ammi-Joan Paquette for taking a chance on me. Your gentle guidance has helped me to gain confidence, learn resilience, and witness firsthand the value of hard work.

Huge thanks to super editor Katherine Jacobs for urging Josie, Fox, and Mason to solve their own problems. They are better people because of it.

Thanks to the talented writers at EMU's Debuts for their unconditional support and permission to be vulnerable.

And thank you to Michael O. Tunnell, whose class many years ago helped me find my way back to children's literature. I owe him big-time.